Her heart beat faster with his every word.

She wanted to argue that he was only trying to make her uncertain of her own conclusions, but there was something in his eyes as he looked at her now...something that dared her to ignore his words.

He shrugged. "In retrospect I suppose it was the perfect plan for getting away with murder. No murder weapon to prove I planned the act. No evidence at all to suggest anything but an accident. And the coup de grâce—half a dozen witnesses watched my frantic efforts to save my wife in that operating room."

Bella adjusted the strap of her bag on her shoulder. "Good night, Dr. Pierce."

She walked out without looking back.

He closed the door behind her without saying more.

Whatever he was hiding, it wasn't murder.

She would bet her career on that assessment.

The trouble was, it wasn't her career she was wagering...it was her life.

SIN AND BONE

USA TODAY Bestselling Author
DEBRA WEBB

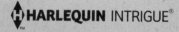
HARLEQUIN INTRIGUE®

This book is dedicated to Chicago, one of my favorite cities and the home of the Colby Agency!

ISBN-13: 978-1-335-63920-2

Sin and Bone

Copyright © 2018 by Debra Webb

Recycling programs
for this product may
not exist in your area.

Printed in U.S.A.

® www.Harlequin.com

Debra Webb is the award-winning *USA TODAY* bestselling author of more than one hundred novels, including those in reader-favorite series Faces of Evil, the Colby Agency and the Shades of Death. With more than four million books sold in numerous languages and countries, Debra's love of storytelling goes back to childhood on a farm in Alabama. Visit Debra at www.debrawebb.com.

Visit the Author Profile page at Harlequin.com.

CAST OF CHARACTERS

Dr. Devon Pierce—A brilliant surgeon and the creator of the Edge, the country's most state-of-the-art emergency department. Someone wants revenge against Devon and will use anything—even his dead wife—to get it.

Isabella Lytle—Bella has spent many years as a police detective and now as a Colby Agency investigator. She will do whatever necessary to protect the client. But can she protect herself from the sexy as hell surgeon?

Mariah and Richard Sutter—Devon's oldest friends, but he isn't sure he can trust them any longer. One of them may want him dead.

Lacon Traynor—Bella's backup at the Colby Agency. Traynor is a top-notch investigator.

Victoria Colby-Camp—The head of the prestigious Colby Agency.

Detectives Corwin and Hodge—Chicago PD is working overtime to solve this bizarre mystery, but the bodies just keep piling up.

Chapter One

The Edge Emergency Department, Chicago Monday, June 4, 5:30 p.m.

Dr. Devon Pierce listened as administrators from more than a dozen hospitals in metropolitan areas across the nation bemoaned the increasing difficulty of maintaining emergency departments. Once the opening discussion concluded, Devon was the featured speaker.

He rarely agreed to speak to committees and groups, even in a teleconference, which was the case today. His participation required only that he sit in his office and speak to the monitor on his desk. He much preferred to remain focused on his work at the Edge. There were times, however, when his participation in the world of research and development was required in order to push his lagging colleagues toward the most advanced medical technologies. Emergency treatment centers like the Edge were the future of emergency medicine. There was no better state-of-the-art facility.

Devon had set his career as a practicing physician aside and spent six years developing the concept for the center's prototype before opening it in his hometown of Chicago. The success of the past year provided significant evidence that his beliefs about the future of emergency rooms were correct. This would be his legacy to the work he loved.

The subject of cost reared its inevitable and unpleasant head in the ongoing discussion as it always did. How could a person measure the worth of saving a human life? He said as much to those listening eagerly for a comment from him. All involved were aware, perhaps to varying degrees, just how much his dedication to his work had cost him. He'd long ago stopped keeping account. His work required what it required. There were no other factors or concerns to weigh.

Half an hour later, Devon had scarcely uttered his closing remarks when the door to his office opened. Patricia Ezell, his secretary, silently moved to his desk. She passed him a note, probably not containing the sort of news he wanted if her worried expression was any indicator, and it generally was.

You're needed in the OR stat.

"I'm afraid I won't be able to take any questions. Duty calls." Devon severed his connection to the conference and stood. "What's going on?" he asked as he closed a single button on his suit jacket.

Patricia shook her head. "Dr. Reagan rushed a patient into surgery in OR 1. He says he needs you there."

Ice hardened in Devon's veins. "Reagan is well aware that I don't—"

"He has the surgery under control, Dr. Pierce. It's…" Patricia took a deep breath. "The patient was unconscious when the paramedics brought her in. Her driver's license identifies her as Cara Pierce."

A spear of pain arrowed through Devon, making him hesitate. He closed his laptop. "Few of us have a name so unique that it's not shared with others." There were likely numerous Cara Pierces in the country. Chicago was a large city. Of course there would be other people with the same name as his late wife. This should be no surprise to the highly trained and, frankly, brilliant members of his staff.

"One of the registration specialists browsed the contacts list in her cell phone and called the number listed as Husband."

Devon hesitated once more, this time at the door. His secretary's reluctance to provide whatever other details she had at her disposal was growing increasingly tedious. "Is her husband en route?"

Patricia cleared her throat. "Based on the number in her contacts list, her husband is already here. The number is *yours*." She held out his cell phone. "I took the call."

Devon stared at the thin, sleek device in her hand. He'd left his cell with Patricia for the duration of the teleconference. He hated the distracting vibration of an incoming call when he was trying to run a teleconference. Normally he would have turned it off and that would have been it, but he was expecting an important work call—one that he would pause his teleconference to take if necessary. So he'd assigned Patricia cell phone duty with instructions to interrupt him only if that call came in, or if there was a life-and-death situation.

He reached for it now.

"Thank you, Patricia. Ask the paramedic who brought her in to drop by my office when he has a break."

The walk from his office in the admin wing to the surgery unit took all of two minutes. One of the finely tuned features of the Edge design was ensuring that each wing of the emergency department was never more than two to three minutes away from anything else. A great deal of planning had gone into the round design of the building with the care initiation front and center and the less urgent care units spanning into different wings around the circle. Straight through the very center, the rear portion of the design contained the more urgent services, imaging and surgery. Every square foot of the facility was designed for optimum efficiency. Each member of staff was carefully chosen and represented the very best in their field.

As he neared the surgery suite, he considered what his secretary had told him about the patient. The mere idea was absurd. There'd been a mistake. A mix-up of some sort.

Cara.

His wife was dead. He'd buried her six years and five months ago.

Devon moved into the observation area where all three operating rooms could be viewed. He touched the keypad and the black tint of the glass that made up the top half of the wall all the way around the observation area cleared, allowing him to see inside and those in the OR to see him. Two of the rooms were empty. One held Cara Pierce.

The patient's hair was covered with the usual generic cap, preventing him from distinguishing the color. Most of her face was obscured by the oxygen mask. He turned on the audio in OR 1.

"Evening, Dr. Pierce," Reagan said without glancing up, his hands moving in swift, perfectly orchestrated movements that were all too familiar to Devon.

"Dr. Reagan." Devon's fingers twitched as he watched the finely choreographed dance around the patient. His life had revolved around saving lives for so long that his entire body was finely tuned into that instinctive rhythm.

"Splenic rupture. Concussion but no bleeding that we've found." Reagan remained focused on the video screen as he manipulated the laparoscopic instruments to resect and suture the damaged organ. "She'll be a little bruised and unhappy about the small surgical scars we'll leave behind but, otherwise, she should be as good as new before you know it."

Five or ten seconds elapsed before Devon could respond or move to go. "Watch for intracranial hemorrhaging." He switched off the audio, darkened the glass once more and walked away.

A weight, one that he had not felt in years, settled on his chest. His wife had died of intracranial hemorrhaging. There had been no one to save her and his efforts had been too little too late. The old ache twisted inside him.

But this woman—who shared Cara's name—was not his wife.

Devon drew in a deep breath and returned to his office. Patricia glanced up at him as he passed her desk but he said nothing. With his office door closed, he moved to the window overlooking the meticulously manicured grounds surrounding the facility. Trees and shrubs were precisely placed amid the expanse of asphalt, lending a welcoming, pleasing appearance. He'd insisted on extensive research for design purposes. What aspects would make the family members of patients feel more at home? What could be done to set a soothing tone for patients? A patient's outlook and sense of well-being and safety were immensely important to healing.

Devon stared at nothing in particular for a long while. When his mind and pulse rate had calmed sufficiently, he settled behind his desk. A couple of clicks of the keyboard opened the patient portal. He pulled up the chart for the Caucasian female he'd observed in surgery. He surveyed the injuries listed as well as the paramedic's comments. The kinds of injuries she had suffered were alarmingly similar to those his late wife had suffered in the car accident that had taken her life.

Pierce, Cara Reese, thirty-seven. Her address

was listed as the Lake Bluff residence Devon had built for his late wife more than a decade ago...the house he had inhabited *alone* for the past six-plus years.

He scrolled down the file to a copy of her driver's license.

His breath trapped in his lungs.

Blond hair, blue eyes. Height five-six, weight one-ten. Date of birth, November 10—all the statistics matched the ones that would have been found on Cara's license. But it was the photo that proved the most shocking of all. Silky blond hair brushed her shoulders. Mischief sparkled in her eyes.

The woman in the photo was Cara. His Cara.

Devon was on his feet before his brain registered that he had pushed up from his chair. The DMV photo was the same one from the last time his wife renewed her license eight years ago. As if that September morning had happened only yesterday, he recalled vividly when she realized her driver's license had expired. She'd been so busy planning another trip before the holidays were upon them she'd completely forgotten. He'd teased her relentlessly.

His chest screamed for oxygen, forcing him to draw in a tight breath. The name could certainly be chalked up to pure coincidence. Even the physical characteristics and the shared birthday. The photo…that was an entirely different story.

A rap on his door pulled him back to the present. Devon reluctantly shifted his attention there. Why wasn't Patricia handling visitors? He needed time to untangle this startling mystery. At the sound of another knock, he called, "Come in."

The door opened and a young man stuck his head inside. "You wanted to see me, Dr. Pierce?"

Devon didn't recognize the face but the uniform was as familiar as his own reflection, maybe more so since he hadn't scrutinized himself in a mirror in years. More than six, to be exact. The contrasting navy trousers and light blue shirt marked his visitor as a member of the Elite Ambulance service. The identifying badge above the breast pocket confirmed Devon's assessment. *The paramedic.*

"You brought in the female patient from the automobile accident?"

He nodded. "My partner and I. Yes, sir. It appeared to be a one-car accident on the Kennedy Expressway near Division. It was the strangest thing."

Devon gestured to the pair of chairs in front of his desk and the young man took a seat. The badge clipped onto his pocket sported the name Warren Eckert. "Strange in what way, Mr. Eckert?"

Devon lowered into his own chair as Eckert spoke. "Nobody witnessed the accident. There was a sizable dent on the front driver's-side fender, but nothing to suggest an accident capable of causing the kind of injuries the patient sustained."

"What kind of vehicle was she driving?"

"A brand-new Lexus. Black. Fully loaded." Eckert whistled, long and low. "Sharp car for sure."

Cara had driven a Lexus. Devon had bought it for her on her last birthday before she died.

"Do you recall seeing anything in the vehicle besides your patient? Luggage perhaps, or a briefcase?"

Eckert shook his head. "I don't remember. Sorry."

"What about the officers investigating the scene?" Obviously the police had been there, probably before Eckert arrived.

"Joe Telly was the only cop on the scene. He called us before he called backup."

"The woman was not conscious when you arrived?"

"No, sir."

"Was she able to speak to the officer before your arrival?" Devon's instincts were humming. How had a woman involved in such a seemingly minor accident been injured so severely?

"She was unconscious when Telly pulled over to check on her."

"How would you describe the woman?" Devon thought about the photo on the driver's license. "I'm sure you concluded an approximate age and such."

The other man nodded. "Blond hair, blue eyes. Medium height. Kind of thin. Midthirties, I'd say."

"Well dressed?" Her clothes had been removed before surgery and very little of her body had been visible on the operating table.

Eckert nodded slowly. "She was wearing a dress. A short black one. Like she might have been headed to a party or dinner out or something. Not the kind of outfit you'd wear to work unless you're a hostess in an upscale restaurant or something like that."

"Thank you, Mr. Eckert." Devon stood. "I appreciate your time."

"Do you know her?"

The rumor had already made the rounds. "No. I'm afraid I don't."

When the paramedic had exited the office, Devon pulled up the record on this Cara Pierce...this woman who could not be his wife.

Preliminary tox screen showed no drugs. And yet if there was no intracranial hemorrhaging, why had she still been unconscious when she arrived at the ER? Remaining unconscious for an extended period generally indicated a serious injury, illness or drug use.

Devon picked up his cell phone and made the call he should have made weeks ago. When she answered, he dived straight into what needed to be said without preamble. "Victoria, I was mistaken. I will require your services after all."

His old friend Victoria Colby-Camp agreed to have her investigator meet him at his residence at eight tonight.

Devon ended the call and tossed his phone onto his desk. Last month, someone had left him an ominous message right here in his office. At first, he'd been determined to have the Colby Agency look into the issue. It wasn't every day that someone who knew how to best his security system dropped by his office and left such a bold message.

I know what you did.

But then he'd decided to drop it. Why stir up his painful past? He knew what he had done. Why allow anyone else to delve into that unpleasant territory?

If the man who'd left him that message

was trying to reach him again, he'd certainly prompted Devon's attention this time.

What better way to send a message than to resurrect the dead?

way, trying to reach him wouldn't be overthinking. Devon's attention was timely.

What better way to send a message than to resurrect the dead?

Chapter Two

Arbor Drive, Lake Bluff, 8:00 p.m.

Isabella Lytle was surprised when the gate to the Pierce property opened without her having to buzz the enigmatic owner for admittance. Instead, the instant her car nosed up to the entrance, the towering iron gates parted and opened wide for her.

She rolled up the long drive, coming to a stop in front of the palatial home. Bella shook her head. She never liked to judge anyone, but Dr. Devon Pierce grated on her somehow. She'd never met the man in person but she had studied his background until she knew it by heart. Victoria had first assigned Bella his case one month ago, but then Dr. Pierce had decided he didn't need the agency's assistance after all.

That should have been the end of it.

But it wasn't.

Even before this latest call for assistance,

Bella had not been able to stop attempting to dissect the man. What made him who he was? What event or events in his childhood and then as an adult had narrowed his focus to a singular purpose—his work? What secrets did he keep? The man had secrets, Bella had no doubt.

The many photos she'd discovered of him on Google sucked her into his world. She knew the clothes he wore, the way he held himself. In recent years, he'd attended endless fund-raisers seeking support for his development of the emergency department of the future. Urbane and sophisticated was the best way to describe his style and the way he carried himself. Beautiful women with money flocked to him as if he were the most eligible bachelor in Chicago, which he probably was. On top of everything else, he was intensely handsome and mysterious.

That was the part that kept reeling her in.

She closed her eyes and gave her head a little shake. Her need to figure him out had become a bit of an obsession.

She forced the thoughts away as her gaze swept over the mansion that would be more suited for a royal estate in England. Who needed twenty-six thousand square feet of living space? A six-car garage? Not to mention an ostentatious fountain perched right in the middle of the parking courtyard. Her eyes rolled upward as she climbed out of her practical sedan. No one. Especially not a man who lived alone. Maybe he was attached to it since he'd lived here with his wife. The estate was an hour's drive from his work in the city. Was this his way of escaping the twelve-to sixteen-hour days?

Was this his hiding place?

Five acres loaded with lots of trees and lush landscaping backed up to Lake Michigan. The main part of the house was large enough but then it winged off on both sides, extending along the manicured grounds, eventually connecting to triple-car garages on either side of the drive, creating a sort of fortress. The iron-and-brick fence was at least twelve feet high and stretched as far as the eye could see, disappearing into the dense woods.

"Lovely." She made the assessment grudgingly with a heavy dose of reluctance. The house was undeniably, extravagantly attractive. Really, it was. She shouldered her bag and shoved her car door shut as she sent a final glance back at the massive gates that had already closed. Dusk had settled, awakening the discreet and well-placed landscape lighting. Did he have the interior lights on timers as well? Every light in the house appeared to be spilling through the windows to greet her.

"I'd hate to pay your electric bill, Dr. Pierce."

She exhaled a big breath and decided she'd dawdled long enough. The cobblestone was damp beneath her shoes from the early-evening rain. Three steps up and she was at the front door.

Victoria, her employer, had sensed Bella's strong reaction to this client. Bella had assured Victoria that she could handle Devon Pierce. The real question in Bella's mind was whether or not Pierce could handle her. To do her job, she would need his cooperation. Not in a million years could she see him cooperating on the necessary level. He was accustomed to being in control...of keeping his secrets. Pierce was a man who preferred doing things his way.

As brilliant as he was, he couldn't be the best at everything. If that was possible, he wouldn't need the Colby Agency's help now.

A part of her—one she intended no one to ever see—wanted him submissive on every level. Chasing away the notion and bracing for the icy glower for which he was known, she pressed the doorbell, listened as it chimed through the house. The door opened and she stared at the man from her numerous Google searches. To her dismay, he was even hotter in person than he was on the computer screen.

She stood under his scrutiny and felt her temper rising. His gaze roved over her, head to toe and back. She'd taken great care with what she chose to wear tonight. A navy skirt, the hem landing just above her knees, and the matching jacket. Her favorite silk shell with its high neckline in the same dark blue color. She never wore heels. At five-nine, she'd always preferred flats. A good pair of shoes with rubber soles and sturdy straps had served her well.

Deep inside she fully comprehended that she would need every part of her professional armor to protect her from his dark lure. She was well aware that her obsession with him hovered on a very narrow ledge. One wrong move and she would slip.

Even as the warning echoed in her brain, her gaze swept over his handsome face. Square jaw darkened by the stubble of a day's beard growth, dark blue eyes analyzing her even as she did the same. He wore a tailored charcoal suit, probably silk. A paler gray shirt peeked from between the lapels of the jacket. He had dispensed with his tie and left a couple of buttons undone. The platinum cuff links remained nestled at the center of his perfectly folded French cuffs. Bella suspected this was as relaxed as he allowed himself to be in front of company.

"Ms. Lytle." He opened the door wider in invitation.

She concentrated her attention on the details of his home rather than on the man. This was the one aspect of Dr. Devon Pierce that remained private. Though there had been plenty of photos of the exterior of the home on the internet, there was none of the interior.

Black and white marble flowed across the floor in a diamond pattern. The walls as well as the ornate trim were coated in an old-world white paint, the aged matte finish an elegant contrast to the glossy floors. A chandelier drenched in crystal hung twelve or so feet overhead. The rich, ornate mahogany table to the left and the cushioned gray bench to the right lent a warm hue to the boundless canvas of sleek black and white.

"I have coffee waiting," he announced.

She nodded. "Lead the way, Doctor."

The large entry hall flowed straight ahead. Some twenty or so feet from the front door, the hall parted to the right and left. On each side, a grand staircase led up to the second level. A wide door beneath the staircase on the right provided a glimpse of the kitchen—opulent wood cabinetry, acres of sleek granite and an expansive wall of windows. The double doors to her far left were closed. A library or his office, she supposed.

Moving straight ahead, the entry hall progressed into a truly stunning great room. The whitewashed walls soared to a vaulted ceiling, complete with rustic wood beams that looked as though they might have held up a bridge somewhere in the Mediterranean in another century. The stone fireplace was huge. The marble floors of the entry hall had given way to gleaming hardwood. The furnishings were upholstered in sophisticated burgundies and golds. To soften the hard surfaces, a classic Persian rug was spread over the center of the room, the burgundy and gold yarn so muted it had surely been washed out by decades of wear in a castle somewhere.

Whatever charm the man lacked in demeanor had been infused into his home. The place was utterly breathtaking. Massive and yet somehow intimate. Nothing like the cool, distant man.

Two sofas faced each other in the center of the room. The silver coffee service sat on the cocktail table between them. As Bella settled onto the edge of one of the sofas, she shifted her gaze and full attention to him. Not an easy feat with so many striking pieces of art she'd only just noticed on the walls.

"Please, have a seat," he said, his voice as terse as it had been when he answered the door. "Do you take cream or sugar?"

"Black is fine, thank you."

She wondered if there were half a dozen housekeepers and a couple of cooks hidden somewhere in the house. God only knew how many gardeners the property required. She glanced around. Surely a member of staff lurked about someplace. She couldn't imagine Devon Pierce using his skilled surgeon's hands to perform such a menial task as preparing coffee.

Former surgeon, she amended. Though his license and hospital privileges and credentials remained in place, he did not routinely practice medicine.

He placed a cup and saucer in front of her, the rich black coffee steaming. Vintage china, she noted. His wife must have been a collector. He poured himself a cup and sat down on the sofa opposite her.

"Victoria tells me you're very good at solving mysteries." He sipped his coffee.

"I'm very good at seeing the details others often miss." The coffee warmed her. From the moment she'd stepped into the house, she'd felt cold. *Liar.* Meeting the man she'd been cyberstalking had sent her temperature rising. *Fool-*

ish. "I spent seven years with the Alabama Bureau of Investigation. I never failed to solve the case I was assigned."

He seemed to consider her answer for a time, his eyes probing hers as if he intended to confirm every word by looking directly inside her soul.

"You graduated from the prestigious University of Alabama with a psych undergraduate degree and a master's in criminal justice," he continued. "Two years as a victim counselor with Birmingham PD and the FBI wanted you but you chose the ABI over the better opportunity."

There it was. That arrogance she instinctively understood would be a part of his personality. She had zero tolerance for it. "The FBI isn't better, Dr. Pierce. It's merely larger with a broader jurisdiction. The work I did for the ABI was immensely important. Had I chosen the FBI, I would have spent a great deal of time working toward the opportunity to be a field investigator. Instead, I went straight to the work that I wanted to do—solving crime in the field."

He set his coffee aside. "I appreciate a stellar résumé, Ms. Lytle, and yours is quite good. But I always look at the person behind the credentials. The heart of the person begins with their roots."

For the first time since she was eighteen, Bella felt the heat of shame rush along her nerve endings. The idea that this man held that much power over her further flustered her. "Not everyone is born into the perfect scenario for who and what they want to become, Dr. Pierce. Some of us had to fight our way out of where we were before we could reach where we wanted to be."

"Your father murdered your mother when you were ten and your thirteen-year-old sister shot and killed him in self-defense," he stated as if she had said nothing at all. "According to the police reports, he was coming at you next and your sister protected you." He studied her a long moment. "The reports also said that the two of you couldn't keep your stories straight. In the end, you seemed to agree with whatever your older sister said."

The blast of a shotgun echoed in Bella's brain followed by screaming…so much screaming. She gathered every ounce of self-control she possessed to prevent her hands from shaking when she carefully set the cup and saucer on the table. "That's right." She held his gaze without flinching. "My father was an alcoholic with a mean streak a mile wide. It would have served my mother far better if she had blown his head off long before he decided to wash his hands of the three of us. My sister was forced to protect us when our mother failed."

Unfortunately, their mother had been weak. Bella blinked once, twice. So weak.

He stared at her for a long time. Pierce was forty-five, ten years her senior, but he didn't look more than forty. His dark brown hair was thick and trimmed in a distinguished yet fashionable style. A few strands of gray had invaded the lush color at his temples. Blue eyes, the color of the sea. Chiseled jaw with a nose that was ever so slightly off center, probably from the car accident when his wife was fatally injured. He'd suffered a broken nose, a fractured jaw and collarbone as well as a gash in the head. Despite his rigorous work schedule, he kept his tall, lean body in excellent condition. She imagined the female nurses and doctors on his staff spent plenty of time discussing the handsome administrator. Particularly since he was single.

Sadly his personality reportedly left a great deal to be desired.

"You narrowly avoided foster care," he went on with his well-prepared monologue of her early history, "but an estranged aunt, your mother's sister, came forward to whisk the two of you to Mobile. At sixteen, your sister dropped out of high school and took a job at a local hair salon. She married and had three children by the time she was twenty. If I counted accurately, she's on husband number five now. You didn't appear very happy in school either. The school counselor documented bruises on several occasions. She listed you as withdrawn and lacking the ability to make friends. Child services were called to your home on more than one occasion."

The shame faded and fury took its place, igniting a blaze that rushed through her veins. "My aunt had rigid religious and disciplinarian views. As for the other, most children go through times in school when making friends is difficult."

Bella had nothing else to say about that part of her life. Her aunt hadn't really been the problem. It was her husband. Bella was fairly confident he got off on beating her and her sister. The slightest infraction required a trip to the woodshed. After her sister left, Bella had tolerated his beatings for a couple more years. Eventually, she'd had enough and she'd got her hands on the ax and threatened to kill him the same way she and her sister had killed their mean-ass daddy. From that point forward, they'd had an agreement of sorts. He didn't touch her and she didn't cut off his head in his sleep. He never touched her again.

Funny how the tendency to choose the wrong kind of man seemed to run in families sometimes. Her mother, her aunt and then her sister. The three looked right over a nice guy and went for the jerk every time.

Bella never intended to allow a man to rule her. *Never.* If Dr. Pierce was under the impression that his extensive knowledge of her past would somehow put her off, he was mistaken. Her past wasn't something she cared to discuss and, frankly, it still embarrassed her to some degree, but this man would need a lot more than humiliating backstory to undermine her determination or her confidence.

Pierce stared at her for a full minute before he spoke again. "My wife died six years and five months ago. My hands were inside her body when her heart stopped beating. I did everything humanly possible to stop the hemorrhaging but I couldn't. She died on the operating table in a hospital that didn't have the proper equipment or the necessary staff. The only surgeon within an hour of the hospital couldn't get there fast enough because of the record-breaking snowstorm that had hit the area. I was the only chance she had of surviving and I failed. I have no idea why someone would use her to rattle me now, but that's precisely what happened today."

Victoria had briefed Bella on the incident. According to her employer's second conversation with Pierce today, he'd examined today's patient after she was placed in the ICU. She had blond hair and pale blue eyes, like his late wife. Similar build. But she was, of course, not his wife. Her face was different though there were definite similarities. Shoe size was wrong. Her fingers weren't as long as Mrs. Pierce's had been.

Not that there had ever been any question. The point was that someone had gone to a great deal of trouble to find a woman who, on first look, greatly resembled Cara Pierce.

"You were able to speak with her." It wasn't a question. Victoria had told Bella as much. She simply wanted to watch his reaction as he answered.

"Briefly. She claimed not to know her name or mine. She couldn't say where her home was or what had happened to her."

"Which could be as a result of her injuries," Bella suggested.

"It's possible but doubtful, in my opinion. There are also certain drugs that can produce the same effect. We're running new screens for those substances."

"Did you tell the police?" Bella knew he had not. She'd spoken to a contact at Chicago PD and nothing else had come in about the accident. As far as the police knew, the woman hit the guardrail. The accident was her fault. No alcohol in her blood. She would survive and the only property damage was her own.

"No, I haven't spoken to the police about the matter." He crossed his arms over his chest in a classic defense gesture. "Since the situation is obviously very personal, I intend to conduct my own investigation first."

Bella wasn't surprised. He wasn't the sort of man to turn over control of something so extremely personal unless he had no other choice. "You do realize that legally you have an obligation to inform the police about the patient's situation."

Another of those long staring sessions came next. Finally, he said, "I do and I will, when I'm ready."

"This is your dime, Dr. Pierce, so we'll play your way until I am compelled to take a different tactic. If at any time I feel the woman in that hospital room is vulnerable to the situation in some way, I will go to the police myself."

"I've assigned security to her room," he said, his tone flat. "She's completely safe."

"As long as we're clear on that point."

"We're quite clear, Ms. Lytle."

She straightened her back, squared her shoulders. "Is there anything else you should tell me before we begin?"

He shook his head, the move so slight she would not have noticed had she not been watching him so closely. "Nothing at all."

Something else Bella had learned during ten years of investigative work, seven at the ABI and three with the Colby Agency, was that when a man could look you straight in the eye and lie without a single tell, he was dangerous.

"Tell me about your enemies, Dr. Pierce."

"When I first began the development phase of the Edge, two years before my wife was killed, I had a couple of partners. Jack Hayman and Richard Sutter. Both eventually fell off the project." One corner of his mouth lifted as if he might smile. "Jack knew basically nothing about what I was doing. He simply wanted to invest part of his vast fortune in something useful."

"What about Richard Sutter?"

Pierce lifted one shoulder in a negligible shrug. "Our parting was less than amiable. He filed several lawsuits but all were dismissed as frivolous."

"Less than amiable" was a vast understatement. "He suffered tremendous financial losses when the two of you severed your business relationship."

A single nod. "Our visions for the project turned out to be vastly different. Severing the relationship was his choice, not mine."

Bella held back the laugh that tickled her throat but she couldn't completely hide the smile. "My assessment of those events is that you left him no other choice."

He stood. "There are always choices, Ms. Lytle. Perhaps limited, but choices nonetheless. I think I'll have something stronger than the coffee. Would you like a drink?"

"The coffee is fine."

She watched as he crossed the room, then opened a cabinet that revealed a bar lined with mirrors and glass shelves. He reached for a bottle of bourbon and poured a significant serving into a glass. His every move was measured, elegant, like the suit he wore.

Bella had read many articles about Pierce before tragedy sent his life on a different path. She'd even watched a couple of television interviews. Dr. Devon Pierce had been a real Chicago hero at Rush University Medical Center. He'd smiled often in the interviews. He'd spoken like a man determined to help others…

determined to do good. He and two partners were developing a new kind of ER model. He had been a man with a mission. A happy man.

This was not the same man. He'd resigned from his position as head of surgery at Rush. He'd become completely obsessed with his mission to create a better ER. He'd withdrawn from society beyond the necessary appearances at fund-raisers. But he had completed his mission. His prototype, the Edge, was an unparalleled emergency department dedicated to his late wife.

When he'd taken his seat once more, she asked, "Assuming his goal is to ruin you or perhaps worse, do you believe Mr. Sutter would go to these extremes to have his vengeance?"

"Richard is an extremely intelligent man with vast resources. He certainly possesses the means to carry out such an elaborately planned plot, but I would prefer to think not. Yet here we are." He sipped his drink.

Bella watched him savor the taste that lingered on his lips. Her throat parched and she had to look away. "You knew the man—like a brother, you claimed in one of the interviews I watched. Would he want to simply damage your reputation? Or is he capable of far worse?"

That blue gaze trapped hers once more.

"Powerful men rarely have set boundaries, Ms. Lytle."

She didn't have to ask if he fell into that same category. "Would he overstep the bounds of the law? Risk criminal charges and perhaps jail time?" As Pierce pointed out, setting up a woman who resembled his wife, complete with similar physical injuries, and delivering her in such a way as was done today was not a small thing. And certainly not one that was legal under any circumstances.

"I believe that may be the case."

"Was a lack of resources why he didn't come after you before? Five years is quite a while to wait for revenge." Sutter and Pierce had broken their partnership five years ago. Sutter had seemingly fallen off the face of the earth until about eighteen months ago. Bella had tracked his return back that far. He stayed out of the public eye these days.

"His resources took a hit when our association ended but he was far from devastated financially," Pierce explained. "It was likely the failed legal steps and the cancer that kept him from making a move like this before. Rumor is he found a private hospital in some country not burdened by the FDA's restraints to seek treatment. I have no idea how long he was out of the country."

A near-death experience like surviving cancer often changed a person's priorities. It was possible that survival had sent Sutter on his own mission. "This might be the most important question I ask you tonight, Dr. Pierce," she warned. "Does Sutter have a legitimate reason to want revenge?" She waited, watched his face, his eyes.

One, two, three seconds elapsed. He downed another sip of bourbon. "Yes."

"All right." Bella appreciated that it hadn't been necessary to drag that answer out of him. More than that, she was grateful he answered honestly. "Does he have some sort of information or evidence that could hurt you?" After all, the message left in Pierce's office had been pretty clear: *I know what you did.*

"Professionally, no."

"What about personally?" Bella waited, suddenly unable to breathe.

He finished off the bourbon before meeting her gaze. "He believes I killed my wife."

There was an answer she hadn't expected. "Does he have tangible evidence or probable cause to believe you wanted your wife dead?"

Bella was certain her heart didn't beat while she waited for him to answer.

"Have you ever loved something so much

you would do anything to possess it and, once it was yours, to keep it?"

His words were spoken so softly, she'd had to strain to hear. As for his question, if she was completely honest she would confess that she felt exactly that way about her work. Her career defined her. There was nothing else. Her sister and she rarely talked, never visited each other. Basically she had no family. No real love life. Her career—her professional reputation—was everything. She would do anything within the law to keep it.

"I suppose so," she said at last.

"I loved my wife, Ms. Lytle." His fingers tightened on the empty glass. "More than anything. I thought giving her everything her heart desired was enough, but it wasn't. She wanted more and I didn't see that until it was too late."

"She turned to someone else," Bella supplied. It happened to career-focused—obsessed—people all the time.

He placed his glass on the table next to the deserted coffee. "She did indeed."

"What did you do about that?" The urge to feel sympathy for him hit her harder than it should have.

"Nothing. I ignored it. Hoped it would go away."

An odd answer for a man who prided himself on keeping his life in perfect order. "Was Sutter the other party involved?"

He turned his palms up. "I have no idea. She took that secret with her to her grave."

The idea that Sutter remained Pierce's partner for a while after her death seemed to negate that possibility. "You never hired a private investigator to look into her extracurricular activities?"

"I did not." He cleared his throat. "I had no desire to confirm my suspicions. I loved her. As I said, I hoped if the worst was true that it would pass."

As heartfelt as his answer sounded, Pierce was the sort of man who generally kept tabs on all aspects of his world. Why would he ignore some part he believed to be out of sync, or worse, out of his control completely?

"How did you come to learn that Sutter suspected you killed your wife?" A good deal of time passed before the two ended their partnership. If Sutter truly believed such a thing, why wouldn't he have brought it up sooner? Weeks or months after Cara Pierce died? Particularly if there was a possibility he had been in love with her.

"Perhaps he thought if he stayed close to me that I would eventually confess to him or that he would find some sort of evidence." He stared at the glass as if weighing the prospect of having a second drink. "I really have no idea what he was thinking. Or why he thought it."

"Did he know you were aware of your wife's affair?"

"I assume he did. He would likely see that as a motive for me wanting her dead. Frankly, there is nothing else his message could have meant."

"But your wife died in a hospital after a car crash. What's his theory about how you murdered her under the circumstances?"

Bella had read the reports. The accident was caused by a horrendous snowstorm. As he said before, the nearest hospital was not adequately equipped. There was no one to do the surgery his wife needed. There was only Devon Pierce and he'd had a broken collarbone, a gash in his head requiring twenty stitches, a broken nose and a fractured jaw. He'd refused to allow them to see to his injuries until his wife was stabilized. When no one could help her, he'd tried. He'd just completed the repair to her ruptured spleen when the bleeding in her brain sent the situation spiraling out of control. According to their statements, the medical staff at the hospital had all agreed: there was nothing else Dr. Pierce or anyone on-site could have done.

Nothing to indicate foul play.

Pierce stood again. "I have no answer for that question. I can only presume Sutter has lost his mind. If you have no other questions, I have work to do."

His sixteen-to twenty-hour-a-day work schedule was something else she'd read about the man. "I'll meet you at your office first thing in the morning," she said as she pushed to her feet.

"I'm usually there by seven."

"I'll be there as well," she fired back without hesitation.

They didn't speak as they walked side by side to the front door. Bella's mind kept going back to the seemingly unfounded idea that anyone could think he murdered his wife. Nothing she had read suggested outbursts or trouble handling his temper. She'd investigated her share of domestic violence cases and he didn't fit the profile. The wife, on the other hand, fit the profile of spoiled rich wife perfectly. Not that Bella had discovered anything overly negative about her, but she had a penchant for spending and self-indulgence.

At the door, she couldn't leave without asking again. "This makes no sense. The person coordinating this threat to you, whether Sutter or someone else, is smart." She waited until he met her gaze. "He must have some reason to believe there was foul play on your part." And some reason to think resurrecting Devon Pierce's dead wife would somehow drive him to drastic measures.

There had been an investigation into his conduct as a physician in the situation. Standard procedure. But the extenuating circumstances warranted the steps he had taken that night.

The eyes that had scrutinized her so intently before abruptly looked away. "We made the trip to see her family once a year, so I had been there numerous times. I was aware of the meager health-care services available in the area." He shrugged. "Perhaps he believes I chose a sedan at the rental car agency rather than an SUV equipped with four-wheel drive and then took that particular road in the storm for the very purpose of ensuring an accident. It was the most treacherous, curvy and hilly. But it was also the shortest route. It felt like the right decision at the time."

"Did you choose the sedan?"

He stared at her now. "There were no SUVs available. They'd all been taken. It was either the car or wait for an SUV to be returned. Which, given the weather, could have been hours or days. I'm not a patient man, Ms. Lytle."

She sensed that he wanted to shake her with

his seemingly blunt self-incrimination. "Were the two of you arguing when the accident occurred?"

"Yes." His face tightened. "She wanted me to turn around. I refused. We were almost there. Going back wasn't an option. The road behind us was worse than what lay ahead of us."

Bella still couldn't see it. "Causing an accident is too risky. You couldn't have known her injuries would be any more life-threatening than your own."

"Unless I gave her head a couple of extra bashes against the window to ensure there was sufficient damage and then waited." His gaze narrowed as if he were remembering. "I seem to recall at least two different accounts of what time our car was noticed. The police pressured me for a bit about the timing of my call for help."

Her heart beat faster with his every word. She wanted to argue that he was only trying to make her uncertain of her own conclusions, but there was something in his eyes as he looked at her now...something that dared her to ignore his words.

He shrugged. "In retrospect, I suppose it was the perfect plan for getting away with murder. No murder weapon to prove I planned the act. No evidence at all to suggest anything but an accident. And the coup de grâce—half a dozen witnesses watched my frantic efforts to save my wife in that operating room."

Bella adjusted the strap of her bag on her shoulder. "Thank you for your time, Dr. Pierce. Good night."

She walked out without looking back. He closed the door behind her without saying more.

Whatever he was hiding, it wasn't murder. She would bet her career on that assessment.

Dr. Devon Pierce was a man of contradictions. Warm to his patients. Cold to the outside world. Pretentious and direct...and yet Bella saw an undercurrent of vulnerability and grief.

It was the latter that pulled at her defenses.

She needed to solve this case quickly...or risk falling under Devon Pierce's enigmatic spell.

If she hadn't already.

Chapter Three

Ms. Lytle had been waiting at his office door when he arrived at seven that morning.

Devon had warned her that he had work to do before they proceeded with the investigation. He refused to allow this diversion to distract him. The medical world was watching, scrutinizing every aspect of this facility's performance. The slightest slip could create a major setback. The Edge and all it represented for the future of emergency medicine were far too important to allow anything to get in the way of forward progress.

He had provided Ms. Lytle with the assistant administrator's office. The position was as yet unfilled, so the office was vacant. He was here sixteen or more hours most days and never far away the rest of the time. Perhaps at a later time, he would view the need for an assistant differently. For now, Patricia represented the only assistant he required. In fact, he'd already discussed with her the possibility of upgrading her position from secretary to personal assistant. She had been with him for ten years, first as his secretary at Rush and then during the development stage of the Edge. Patricia had never once let him down.

She had been most unhappy with Ms. Lytle's request for an interview with her this morning. Now, forty-five minutes later, the private investigator had returned to her desk and so far hadn't said a single word to Devon. He stared at the woman seated across from him now. "Patricia Ezell is above reproach. If you insulted her in some way, I would require that you apologize immediately."

A smile lifted Isabella Lytle's inordinately lush lips. At their initial meeting last night, he'd at first thought she wore lipstick but he recognized now that she didn't. Her lips were naturally a deep crimson, full and wide.

"I asked the hard questions, yes, but if Ms. Ezell took offense at any of those questions, that's unfortunate. They were all crucial. The people closest to you represent the greatest danger. Whether by design or accident, they make you vulnerable merely because they have your confidence."

His first instinct was to argue the point but he chose to let it go. She'd already interviewed Patricia. Not another living soul knew him so well. The entire staff at the Edge had been made aware that Ms. Lytle was to be treated with respect and given complete access. "Since there is no one else to interview, what is your agenda for the day?"

He had not expected that she would stay so close. He didn't know what he had expected. Having her study his every move was disconcerting.

Today she wore all black. Black slacks, black jacket, black sweater that hugged her throat. All that was visible of her pale skin was her face and hands. Her dark hair, as dark as the clothes she wore, had been arranged in a French twist. She might have appeared stern or harsh if not for her expressive brown eyes and that voluptuous mouth. There was a kindness, a gentleness about her eyes. Yet she emanated a firm, steady strength that warned she was far from soft.

"Actually, I'd like to interview the woman the police identified as your wife."

A new thread of unease filtered through him. He'd stopped by the woman's—a Jane Doe, for all intents and purposes—room this morning. She'd still been asleep. Security remained at her door 24/7. Until someone claimed her and took her away, he intended to keep her close and protected.

"Very well."

As they exited his office, he noticed that Patricia did not so much as spare a glance toward Ms. Lytle. He would speak to her as soon as this interview was over.

Ms. Lytle walked slightly in front of him. Her stride was confident, determined. His research showed that she was not married, had never been married. No children. Isabella Lytle lived alone on Armitage Avenue in the Lincoln Park area. No previous engagements. No long-term boyfriends or girlfriends.

Before he could quash the thought, he wondered about the woman. Were her most intimate needs kept hidden? A dirty secret she wanted no one to know? His gaze moved down her shapely backside. Or perhaps she was like him—work was her only true companion. Anything else was an afterthought.

They moved around the circular corridor until they reached the quarantine unit. The Edge did not keep patients more than twenty-four hours unless it was necessary to quarantine them until proper care could be arranged. There were overnight beds in the behavioral and senior units, but all other patients were either treated and released or transported to nearby hospitals. The Edge was not intended as anything other than an emergency care facility. Since the woman's true identity had not been determined, there was no next of kin to take her home and no medical necessity to prompt a transfer.

He would, however, need to turn the situation over to the police soon. No matter that she was an impostor and clearly connected to some criminal activity, he could not keep holding her as if she were a prisoner. As some point, the entire matter would need to be turned over to the police.

But not until he was satisfied.

A quick nod to the security guard outside the room and the man took a break. Devon rapped twice on the door before opening it for Ms. Lytle to enter ahead of him. The woman listed as Cara Pierce was awake. She turned in surprise or perhaps in fear as they entered the room.

"Good morning." Ms. Lytle approached her bedside and introduced herself. "I'm Investigator Isabella Lytle and I have a few questions for you."

The woman frowned and then winced. "I don't remember anything." She glanced at Devon. "I've already told you that."

Devon had reviewed her chart this morning. She'd slept well. Had consumed a good portion of her breakfast. Vitals were good. The general symptoms associated with splenic rupture were all but gone. Vision was within normal range. No light-headedness or shock. Beyond the confusion about her identity, all appeared to be well.

Then again, mere confusion rarely included a driver's license and vehicle registration in the wrong name. Obviously the woman was working with someone. Frankly, her brain injury was hardly significant enough to have caused any serious confusion or amnesia. Now that she was stable, there was no reason she shouldn't be able to tell the truth. No other drugs had been found in the follow-up toxicology. Of course, there were a number of drugs that dissipated too quickly to be caught in a tox screen.

"Let's talk about who you are," Ms. Lytle suggested to the woman in the bed. "What is your name?"

The pretend Cara blinked, then looked away. "I don't know."

Ms. Lytle set her bag on the floor and reached inside. She removed a plastic bag somewhat larger than a typical sandwich bag. With her hand inside the bag, she used it like a glove to pick up the plastic cup on the patient's overbed table. Then she pulled the plastic over the cup, successfully bagging it.

With a quick smile at the other woman, Ms. Lytle said, "The police might be able to track down your identity through your fingerprints."

Big blue eyes stared first at Ms. Lytle and then at Devon. "Is that legal?" she asked him. "For her to come into my room and take my fingerprints like that?" She knotted her fingers together. "I haven't done anything wrong."

"Don't you want to know who you are?" Devon braced his hands on the footboard of the bed. "You may have a husband or family worried about you."

She stared directly at him, her blue eyes pooled with tears. Fear, whether real or simulated, glistened there. "You're certain I'm not your wife?"

"No. You are not my wife."

Ms. Lytle placed the commandeered cup into her bag and retrieved a pad and pen. "Why don't we start with whatever you remember before arriving at the ER?"

The woman blinked, stared for a long moment at Ms. Lytle. "I don't remember anything."

Ms. Lytle nodded. "All right, then. We'll see what the police can find. If there are any outstanding warrants or investigations related to your fingerprints, they will discuss those issues directly with you. I wish you a speedy recovery."

The woman, looking decidedly pale against the white sheets, bit her bottom lip as if to hold back whatever words wanted to pop out of her. Ms. Lytle picked up her bag and turned toward the door before hesitating. She studied the other woman for half a minute before she spoke. "You do realize that if someone hired you to pretend to be Cara Pierce that you're a loose end?"

The pretender's eyes grew wider. "I don't understand what you mean."

"When that person—the person who hired you—is finished with whatever game he's playing, you will be an unnecessary risk. We—" she gestured to Devon "—can help you, but we're not going to waste resources on an uncooperative witness."

A frown furrowed across her brow. "Witness?"

Ms. Lytle nodded. "That's what you are. Someone has committed a crime. You obviously know who that someone is, so that makes you a witness, perhaps an accessory. If you willingly participated in that crime, then you'll be charged accordingly—unless you cooperate, in which case the DA might offer you immunity."

"So," she said slowly, "you're a cop."

Isabella Lytle had introduced herself as an investigator. Devon hadn't considered it at the time but the move was an ingenious one.

"Investigator Lytle," he said, saving her the lie, "has been assigned to your case. If you cooperate, she may be able to help you avoid legal charges."

Silence thickened for several seconds before the woman blurted, "I didn't know he was going to try to kill me or I would never have gone along with this crazy scheme." She looked from Devon to Ms. Lytle, her fingers knotted in the sheet. "I thought it was a game."

Ms. Lytle asked, "The man who hired you, do you know his name?"

She shook her head and then winced. Her head no doubt still ached. "He never told me his name. He offered me five thousand dollars and promised there was a bonus if I didn't screw up."

Ms. Lytle reached for her pad and pen once more. "Can you describe the man to me?"

She blew out a big breath, and her blond bangs fluttered. "You're not going to believe this but it was dark in the room where we met. He wouldn't let me turn on the lights. He told me what he wanted, gave me a thousand bucks up front and walked out. Next thing I knew, I was snagged from my regular corner. I don't remember anything after that until I woke up here."

"You're a prostitute, is that correct?" Outrage burst inside Devon. The idea that whoever had done this had taken advantage of someone so vulnerable made him all the angrier.

"A girl's gotta make a living somehow." She straightened the sheet at her waist. Smoothed the wrinkles her nervous fingers had created.

"Where did you and this man meet?" Ms. Lytle asked.

"Over on East Ontario." She fidgeted with the edge of the sheet some more. "A car picked me up and took me to that real fancy hotel over on Michigan Avenue." Her lips trembled into a small smile. "I was thinking that was going to be my lucky day. You know, a big tipper."

"Which hotel?" Ms. Lytle asked.

When the woman had given the name and address of the hotel, Devon demanded, "What can you tell me about his voice? Deep? Did he sound older or younger?"

"Not really so deep. He sounded older than me for sure." She moistened her lips. "His voice was kind of gravelly like he'd spent a lot of years smoking."

"What exactly did he ask you to do?" Devon demanded. He realized he'd taken over the interview but it was his prerogative. Ms. Lytle worked for him, after all. This outrageous situation was about him! Fury twisted sharply inside him.

"He said all I had to do was pretend to be someone else for a day. Easy money. Big money." She shrugged one thin shoulder. "I didn't know I'd be getting hurt and almost die."

"What's your name?" Ms. Lytle asked before Devon could launch his next question.

"Audrey." She stared at her manicured fingernails, anywhere but at the woman questioning her. "Audrey Maynard."

"Audrey," Ms. Lytle began, "you said the hotel room was dark. Did you get any sense of his height or how big or small he was?"

She started to move her head but winced. "Not really. He was sitting in a chair. I could sort of make out his form against the cream-colored chair. He wore dark clothes. He wasn't a big guy. Thin and medium height, I guess."

"Did he wear cologne?"

She thought about that question for a moment. "Yes. Something expensive. I think it was that Clive something or other. I only smelled it a couple other times—once when I was part of a group of girls who attended this secret party with a bunch of really rich guys. The stuff costs like thousands of dollars."

"Clive Christian," Devon said. The woman in the bed as well as Ms. Lytle turned to stare at him. He was well acquainted with the cologne she meant.

"That's it." She pointed at him. "And you. You wear it. I smelled it when you checked on me this morning."

"Did you keep any of the money he gave you?" Ms. Lytle asked. "What was the money in? A bag? A box?"

"It was in a bag. The shiny pink kind like you get from that fancy lingerie place. But I threw it away."

"What did you do with the money?" Ms. Lytle prodded.

"I paid my mother's rent. She was behind. She's sick. Emphysema." She sighed. "It's bad."

Ms. Lytle asked, "Did he contact you again after that?"

"He just said he'd send his car after me when he was ready."

"When did the car come for you?"

"Yesterday morning. It was waiting outside my mother's place when I walked out the door."

"Tell us about the car." Ms. Lytle prepared to jot down the information.

"Black. One of those big sedans you see hauling rich people around but not a limo."

"What about the license plate? Did you see it?" Devon asked.

"No. I'd had a rough night. I was pretty out of it."

"Did you see the driver?" Ms. Lytle inquired before Devon could.

"Yeah. He was white. Midtwenties maybe. Black hair, cut short. Not exactly cute. He looked, you know, indifferent. Wore a black suit. He told me I was to go with him the way I agreed. After I got in the car, he didn't say a word."

"Where did he take you?"

"Damen Silos. He just put me out and drove off. I was still staring after him when someone grabbed me from behind." She frowned. "Wait. Maybe I did see part of the license plate." She called off two numbers. "There were some numbers and then a TX. That's all I can remember."

"Thank you," Ms. Lytle said. "We may have more questions later."

"When will I be able to go home? I'm sure my mom is worried about me. I'm all she's got."

Ms. Lytle looked to Devon.

"Leave the contact information with Ms.

Lytle and we'll see that your mother is informed of your whereabouts."

He walked out of the room. The guard resumed his position next to the door as Devon moved away. How many people knew the cologne he wore? The description of the man who'd hired her was insufficient but there was enough to further convince Devon with whom he was dealing. His former partner Richard Sutter.

Ms. Lytle hurried from the room to catch up with him. "It's time to call in the police, Dr. Pierce. I don't believe she's telling us the whole truth."

When he stalled, she glanced back at the room and the guard stationed there before meeting his impatient glare. "I know when a witness is lying, and for whatever reason, the woman in that room lied with every breath."

He had come to the same conclusion. When he continued to stare in the direction of the room without responding to Ms. Lytle's suggestion, she went on, "At the very least, I should get this cup to a friend of mine who can run the prints. We need to confirm who she is. She has rights and we're walking all over those rights by not bringing in the proper authorities."

His attention shifted to her, fury whipping

through him. "I am well aware of the patient's rights, Ms. Lytle."

"Then you know we have to do something to protect her. I spent far too many years as a cop to ignore the situation. The man who hired her will not want her talking. Victoria and the Colby Agency have a reputation for high standards. I'm not about to let Victoria or the agency down."

"I'm not asking you to let anyone down." He started walking toward his office once more. "She has protection at her door and we're going to do something right now."

She hurried to keep up with his long strides. Though she was five-nine and in excellent physical condition, he stood at six-two and was quite fit himself. He had the advantage physically. He forced away thoughts of testing her physical endurance in all sorts of ways.

As they reached his office, she managed to get ahead of him and to block the door. "Where exactly are we going?"

He reached for patience. "To see the car. Any personal effects may still be in the vehicle. I'd like to see those and the registration."

"Makes sense." She stepped away from the door. "But I'm driving."

C&C Towing, Noon

GEORGE TALBOT, her friend in Chicago's Crime
Scene Processing Unit, had promised to get re-
sults on the prints back to her ASAP. For the
moment, she had let Pierce off the hook about
reporting to PD what they had learned from the
woman who had pretended to be his wife. But
as soon as they'd had a look at any personal
effects in the vehicle, the call would be made.
The TX Maynard had told them about meant
the car was a taxi or other chauffeured vehicle. If they could track down the vehicle and
the driver, they might learn who'd hired him.

"This is it." The tow-truck driver had escorted them into the storage yard, down the
fifth row and seven cars over to where the
Lexus was parked. "Damage isn't so bad. We
have a repair service if you want her fixed.
We're happy to fax an estimate to your insur-
ance company."

"I'll let you know," Pierce said. "At the moment, I'd like to gather my wife's belongings."

The lie rolled off his tongue without the first
flinch or glance away from the man in the sum-
mer-weight coveralls. Bella had barely slept last
night for mulling over their conversation in his
home. Devon Pierce had the poker face down to
a science. It was nearly impossible to determine

what was truth and what was not. Worse, there was something about him that pulled at her. Certainly not his immense charm, she mused. Something deeper…something darker.

Perhaps a darkness similar to the one that lived inside her—a distrust of others so deep and profound that it muddied any personal feelings she might hope to ever develop. Who was she kidding? She had decided long ago that a personal life was too complicated. Work was far easier.

"All rightie, then." The driver tossed the keys to Pierce. "Drop them by on your way out. We don't release the keys or the vehicle until the bill is settled."

Pierce gave him a nod.

When the driver had headed back to his office, Pierce reached for the driver's-side door. Bella stopped him with a hand on his arm. "This car is evidence."

"Be that as it may, I'm having a look in the car." His tone warned there would be no discussion on the subject.

She reached into her bag and dug up a couple of pairs of latex gloves. She passed a pair to him.

He shot her a look. "The fact that you carry gloves around in your bag could be construed as—"

"I'm a private investigator. The last thing I ever want to do is render a piece of evidence unusable in court."

She'd seen more than her share of bumbling detectives do exactly that and the perp ended up getting off on a technicality. Not happening on her watch.

While he settled behind the steering wheel, Bella opened the door to the back seat and had a look there. The small black clutch Maynard—or whoever she was—had with her was brought to the hospital. It had contained the driver's license, lip gloss and a small round makeup mirror. One black high heel lay on the back floorboard. No overnight bag. No trash or spare change. The car looked and smelled brand-new.

"Have a look at this."

Bella withdrew her upper body from the back seat and moved to the driver's door. He held documents he'd taken from the glove box.

"The car was bought—if I'm reading this correctly—yesterday." He passed the paperwork to her. "There's nothing else here except one black shoe."

"The other one is in the back seat." She skimmed the pages. It appeared Cara Pierce had bought the car from the local Lexus dealership yesterday morning. She passed the papers back to him. "Did you check the console between the seats?"

"It's empty."

He peered up at her, blue eyes dark with fury. His lean jaw was taut with that same anger. Someone was using his painful past to get to him. But what was the endgame? That was the part Bella couldn't yet see. Were they trying to discredit him professionally or destroy him personally? The rage in his eyes turned to something even more fierce…something desperate and urgent, something hungry. Bella abruptly realized how close she was standing to him.

Her ability to breathe vanished. "Well." She stumbled back a step from the vee made by the open door of the car. "Let's check the trunk."

He pressed the button on the dash and a *pop* confirmed the trunk had opened. Bella headed that way with Pierce close behind. She struggled to dispel the hum of uncertainty and something like need inside her. The foolish reaction was surely related to her utter inability to sleep last night.

The trunk was empty save a single sheet of lined paper with words scribbled frantically across it. The page looked as if it had been ripped from a notebook. Blood was smeared across the center of it.

Pierce snatched up the page and stared at it.

"Don't touch anything," she warned again. Then she surveyed the trunk once more. Another spot of crimson at the edge of the carpeting snagged her attention. She lifted the carpeting that covered the spare tire area and she stopped.

Blood.

Lots of blood.

Pierce leaned in close, his face far too near to hers. "Ms. Lytle, I believe it's time to call the police now."

Chapter Four

The Edge, 1:55 p.m.

For the second time today, Bella found herself walking briskly to keep up with Pierce's hurried strides. She had to admit, seeing the half dozen Chicago PD cruisers out front was enough to have anyone rushing to see what was going on.

Once the call was made, he'd refused to wait at the tow lot until the police arrived. Bella had almost refused to bring him back and then he'd reached for his cell to order a car. She'd had no choice. As much as she'd felt that legally speaking they needed to wait for the police to take possession of the Lexus, she had known she could not allow Pierce out of her sight. He was at the edge—no pun intended.

Whatever had been on that page—he'd thrust it into his jacket pocket too quickly for her to get so much as a glimpse—it had shaken him.

The paper was evidence and he'd taken it from the scene. He'd put her in an untenable position. Yet her first responsibility was to the client. She couldn't say for a certainty that the paper he'd taken was significant evidence—which would present the one situation in which her obligation to him slipped out of first place. Basically until she knew what was on that page, she needed to focus on protecting the client.

From himself as much as any other threat.

They reached the quarantine unit and the door to Maynard's room was open. The guard was no longer at the door. Bella glanced at Pierce and his face was clouded with that same anger she'd been watching darken his eyes since their conversation with his pretend wife hours ago.

A uniformed Chicago PD officer and two men in suits—detectives, she surmised—were crowded around Maynard's bed.

"What's going on here?" Pierce demanded.

"Dr. Pierce," one of the suits said, "glad you're finally here."

The suit glanced at Bella. "Detective Corwin," he said, then gestured to the other suit. "Detective Hodge."

He didn't introduce the uniform, but his name, Laurence, was on his name tag anyway.

"Investigator Isabella Lytle." She thrust out her hand. "The Colby Agency."

"We have a situation," Corwin said.

"Your patient—" Hodge checked his notes "—Cara Pierce."

"That is not her name," Pierce snapped.

Bella started to speak but Hodge cut her off. "She called 911 and reported that you, Dr. Pierce, had kidnapped her and held her hostage for two months until she escaped yesterday. That running from you is the reason she had the accident. She said you were holding her here at the hospital as well and that she had to get away so she could hide from you."

"What?" Pierce demanded. "We spoke to her—Audrey Maynard—just this morning. She claimed to have been paid by some person she couldn't name or identify to pretend to be my deceased wife. The man who hired her also orchestrated her accident so that she would be brought here. Ask her for yourself."

The suits and the uniform stepped away from the bed. It was empty.

Bella's instincts rocketed to the next level. "How long has she been gone?"

"The call came in to dispatch around noon," Corwin said. "We've been here maybe half an hour." He shifted his gaze to Pierce. "Waiting for you."

"Where's the guard who was stationed at her door?" Pierce demanded.

"We've interviewed him," said Corwin, who seemed to be the lead detective. "He's headed downtown, where we'll question him some more."

"What did the guard say happened?" Bella asked before Pierce could make another demand.

"He says she came to the door demanding a phone. When he refused to provide her with one, she took off down the hall. She snatched a cell phone off the counter at the nurses' station. When we got here," Corwin went on, "she was gone. We've got uniforms crawling all over this place."

Bella held up her hands when Pierce would have bellowed something not in the least helpful. "Take your time, gentlemen. Interview every member of staff if necessary. Ms. Maynard was not a prisoner here. The guard was for her protection since we couldn't determine if there was a further threat to her life. Considering the way she was brought here, we were concerned. As for her sudden disappearance, she can't have gotten far in her physical condition."

"Hold up." Corwin shook his head. "What does all that mean?"

"Why don't we take this discussion to my office?" Pierce suggested. "We'll explain everything."

Corwin instructed Laurence to wait at the abandoned room. He and Hodge followed Bella and Pierce to his office. Patricia glanced up as Pierce warned that he didn't want to be disturbed. She ignored Bella altogether. Apparently she was still unhappy about the questions Bella had asked. There was no help for that.

Once the two detectives were settled in front of Pierce's desk and Bella had taken a seat at a small conference table, Pierce explained the events that had taken place since Maynard's arrival in the ER. He walked them through his interview that morning and the information about the car's license plate and the hotel where she'd met the man who'd hired her. Occasionally he looked to Bella for confirmation. When he reached the part where they looked at the car Maynard had been driving, he allowed Bella to take over.

"The interior of the car appeared fine," she said. "According to the paperwork in the glove box, it was only purchased yesterday. The one troubling issue we noted was the blood in the trunk."

The relief on Pierce's face when she didn't

mention the page he'd tucked into his jacket was palpable. *Protect the client.*

"Ms. Lytle," Hodge said, "the dealership reported that car stolen. We got the call just a little while ago."

"Then the paperwork was forged," Pierce said. "To prevent the officers who responded to the accident from becoming suspicious."

Corwin nodded. "Evidently. We're well aware of who you are, Dr. Pierce. Your work in the community is well noted and our captain warned us to keep the gloves on for this one. The way I hear it, the mayor himself is a personal friend of yours."

"Dr. Pierce wants the truth," Bella interceded. "He wants you to investigate this situation to the best of your ability. A woman was brought to him posing as his deceased wife. Clearly, someone is attempting to besmirch his name and to cause him great personal pain."

"Since we can't question the woman you claim is Audrey Maynard," Corwin began, "we're going to need your full cooperation, Dr. Pierce."

When Pierce would have spoken, Bella held up a hand for him to wait. "Before we proceed, Dr. Pierce has a right to proper counsel, particularly in an unknown situation like this one. If your assertions are accurate, Ms. Maynard and whoever hired her are attempting to frame Dr. Pierce in a very serious crime. Kidnapping is a very grave crime."

Corwin heaved a breath. "First, this is not an assertion. You can listen to the 911 call for yourself. The woman made the statement. She gave the name Layla Devereux."

"That may be her street name," Bella argued. "I'm confident if you take her prints from the cell phone she used or from the room, you'll find that her name is Audrey Maynard." Her friend had sent a text confirming the name and a couple of arrests for solicitation. Bella had the address listed as her home but, under the circumstances, she wasn't giving up that information. She wouldn't compromise the identity of her lab contact—or herself—by telling them she'd already found the information before reporting the crime. These two could figure it out for themselves.

"We have a two-man forensic team en route as we speak," Hodge assured her.

"Don't waste your time investigating me, Detective," Pierce said. "The man who hired this woman, who seriously injured her, is the person you should be looking for. If my associate, Ms. Lytle, and I are correct in our conclusions, Ms. Maynard is very likely in danger. The man behind this, whatever it is, will want to ensure nothing and no one leads back to him."

"Let's talk about your enemies," Corwin suggested.

While Pierce spoke, Bella sent a text to her Colby Agency backup. She wanted someone at the address listed as Maynard's residence just in case she showed up there. Bella sent him a pic she'd snapped of Maynard in the room this morning.

Pierce went through the same paces with the detectives that Bella had put him through last night. The sooner they satisfied the detectives, the sooner they would be on their way.

When enough questions had been asked and answered, Bella took advantage of a pause and asked, "Where did Ms. Maynard claim Dr. Pierce had been holding her these last two months? And how did she escape in a brand-new stolen Lexus with another woman's driver's license in her bag?"

She felt confident the detectives could see the absurdity of the scenario the same as she. Pierce spent sixteen or more hours a day here. He'd said as much and had the staff and security footage to back it up. He'd already asked his security specialist to pull up the feed for all exterior doors and the parking lot to show Maynard's exit. If someone picked her up, maybe the license plate would be captured on the video. Or, at the very least, the make and model of the vehicle.

Corwin looked to Pierce. "She says you kept her in your home. The clothes, the ID with your dead wife's name were things you forced her to use. Furthermore, she said you have a red room and that's where you kept her as your private sex slave."

When Pierce stared blankly at him, Hodge tacked on, "You know, like that movie, *Fifty Shades*."

When Pierce didn't appear able to find his voice, Bella argued, "It sounds as if she did a lot of talking on that call for a woman who wanted out of here for fear that her captor or one of his hirelings would return at any moment."

Pierce glanced at her, a glimmer of appreciation in his gaze.

Corwin nodded. "Definitely. I'm with you. Sounds like a setup." He pressed his lips together and made a noncommittal sound. "But then there's the issue of those rumors that lingered after your wife died."

Bella looked from Corwin to Pierce. His face had closed. No more anger, no more gratitude or uncertainty. The poker face was back. "What are you implying, Detective?"

"The doc knows," Corwin said to Bella rather

than respond to Pierce's demand. "When his wife died, there were rumors that he wanted her dead."

Bella rose from her chair before she realized she intended to do so. "Thank you, Detectives. Dr. Pierce has been through quite enough for today. I'm certain you'll let him know if you have additional questions."

Corwin looked from her to Pierce. "Is that the way you want to play this, Doc?"

Pierce removed a business card from the center drawer of his desk and handed it to Corwin. "Contact my attorney if you have more questions."

The two detectives stood. "If you've got nothing to hide, you needn't be concerned." As he turned away, Corwin paused to survey Bella from head to toe and back. "Be careful, Investigator Lytle. You might find yourself strapped to a leather bed."

When the two had exited the door, Bella closed it. She looked directly at Pierce. "I'm going to assume none of what they're suggesting is true."

Pierce said nothing.

"You know they're going to get a warrant."

Pierce's cool composure slipped, but only for a moment. "A warrant wasn't mentioned. I doubt they'd go to those extremes just yet."

Bella struggled to keep from rolling her eyes. "They aren't going to give you the heads-up— they'll want to catch you off guard. They don't want to risk you hiding or disposing of evidence before they get there. But you can bet a warrant is coming. If they search your house, will they find anything incriminating?"

"Nothing that will connect me to any of this."

His tone was flat, his face giving nothing away.

"Have you ever met Audrey Maynard before?"

"No."

She already knew he had nothing to do with his wife's death, so she wasn't even going there. "Do you have a so-called red room?"

"How is that relevant?"

A spark of anger was back in his eyes.

Holy hell. "When they search your home— and they will—anything that lends credibility to her story will throw up warning signs and warrant further investigation."

She tried to focus on her job instead of Pierce's so-called red room. Suddenly, the short-sleeved silk sweater she'd chosen to wear today felt too thick though it was thin and gauzy. Perspiration rose on her skin. The urge to peel off her jacket was nearly overwhelming. Of all the things she expected to learn about

Dr. Devon Pierce during this investigation, his taste for kink wasn't one of them. She blinked away the images of his lean body, naked save leather handcuffs. She drew in a harsh breath, willed her mind to stop conjuring those erotic mental pictures. "I need you to be open and honest with me, Dr. Pierce. It's the only way I can help you."

"What they will find," he said, forcing her attention back to him, "is personal and irrelevant to this investigation."

Liar.

She closed her eyes and shook her head. "Our time is short. I hope your status in the community and the powerful people with whom you are associated will slow their efforts to get a warrant. That said, I doubt those two will stop until they persuade one judge or the other to sign the warrant. But we'll worry about crossing that bridge when it's in front of us. For now, we're going to visit Audrey Maynard's mother."

A frown furrowed his handsome brow. "You believe she'll talk to us or are you hoping her daughter will be hiding there?"

Bella wanted to believe Devon Pierce was as honest as he was handsome. As much as she hated to admit it, she wasn't immune to his mysterious pull. But her instincts warned her he wasn't being completely truthful. There was more to the story. "I do believe we can gain some amount of cooperation. As for Audrey, it's possible she would risk going to a known location. I suppose it depends on just how scared she is." She grabbed her bag and headed for the door. "Let's go."

The sooner she was out of this office and focused on the investigation, the sooner she could clear her head of the images the detectives' accusations against Pierce had elicited.

His bare skin draped in leather and chains flashed full-size in her mind.

You are in trouble here, Bella.

Deep trouble.

South Bishop Street, 5:00 p.m.

THE MORGAN PARK neighborhood was an old one with plenty of historic bungalows to prove its age. Some parts were undergoing gentrification and others were less fortunate. The small brick bungalow belonging to Olivia Maynard landed somewhere in the middle with its sagging roof begging for attention and picket fence in need of paint while meticulously groomed shrubs and vibrant blooming flowers filled the yard. On the front porch, an array of eclectic pots overflowed with more flowers. A swing and a rocking chair welcomed visitors while at the same time clashing with the iron bars on the windows and the triple dead bolts on the door.

Bella knocked on the door. If they were lucky, they had got here before the police and would have the information they needed before their arrival. She wanted to hear the mother's take on the daughter before her opinion was colored by reality. Pierce stood so close to her that she felt too hot again in her chosen wardrobe. She resisted the urge to step away from him.

Was his closeness an attempt to intimidate her?

No answer at the door. She knocked again and waited, absently rubbing her knuckles. Would Audrey have dared to take off on her own? Had she chosen to completely ignore the warning about being a loose end? Bella hated the idea of her ending up dead. She wouldn't have been the first prostitute to get caught up in a game that led to her demise.

Whoever had hired her to pretend to be Pierce's wife clearly was not playing games.

The shade on the door drew back far enough for someone to peek out. One by one, the dead bolts were released and the door swung open a couple of inches.

"If you're selling something, including religion, I'm not interested." The woman had

blond hair, though her gray roots were starting to show, and blue eyes. Her face was an
older version of her daughter's.

Definitely Audrey's mother.

"Mrs. Maynard?"

The woman looked at Bella and said, "If
you're cops, Audrey's not here. I haven't seen
her for a couple of days."

At least part of that statement was good
news.

"Mrs. Maynard, my name is Isabella Lytle
and this is my associate, Dr. Devon Pierce.
We're here about Audrey."

Her face fell, and fear crept into her eyes. "Is
she all right?"

"Please," Bella urged, "may we come inside?"

The door opened wide in invitation and
Bella breathed a sigh of relief. Inside, her eyes
quickly adjusted to the dim interior. A lamp
sat on a table flanked by two chairs. On the far
wall was a small box-style television perched
on a long narrow table loaded with framed photographs. Across the small room to Bella's left
was a well-loved sofa. A throw and a couple
of pillows were tucked at one end. The part in
the curtains allowed a strip of sunlight to cut
across the worn wood floor.

Hands wringing together, Ms. Maynard sat
down in the chair closest to the television set.

She reached for the oxygen concentrator on the table next to her chair. She put the nasal cannula in place, draped the lines over her ears and inhaled deeply. She closed her eyes and seemed to relax a little.

When she'd opened her eyes, Pierce asked, speaking for the first time, "When was the last time you saw your daughter?"

"Sunday night, I think. She was gone the next morning before I woke up." She shrugged her thin shoulders. "I suppose she could have left in the middle of the night, but she was here when I went to bed Sunday night."

This was really good news. The mother's statement directly contradicted the daughter's assertion against Pierce. Audrey Maynard left her home either late Sunday night or early Monday morning and showed up in the ER on Monday evening. Dr. Pierce's whereabouts, other than the few hours before seven Tuesday morning, could be verified.

Bella pulled the photo she'd taken of Audrey on screen and showed it to Mrs. Maynard. "Is this your daughter?"

Her face crumpled. "Yes. Oh my Lord, is she hurt?"

"She was in an accident," Pierce explained, "but we took care of her injuries."

"So she's all right?" The older woman looked from Pierce to Bella and back.

"She was when we last saw her," Bella explained. "She left the hospital this afternoon and we're concerned for her safety. We believe she may be involved with a dangerous man."

Her mother shook her head. "I knew something was wrong when she paid my house payment for the next two months." She sighed. "This place should have been paid for years ago but I've had to borrow the money for upkeep every now and then. I guess I'll be making payments for the rest of my days."

"We want to help your daughter, Mrs. Maynard," Pierce said. "If she was in trouble, where might she go?"

"She's got lots of friends that do…" She shrugged. "…what she does. But they probably wouldn't tell you a thing if you asked them."

Bella drew a business card from her bag and gave it to Mrs. Maynard. "The police will be visiting you as well, probably today. Tell them anything at all you can remember about whatever your daughter said to you in the past few days. Any friends who might know where she is. Any place she might hide."

She stared at the card for a moment, then asked, "You're a private investigator?"

"Yes, ma'am. I want to find your daughter before anyone who might want to hurt her does."

The lines on the woman's face deepened. "You talk to her friends. They might talk to you since you're not a cop. You can find them over on East Ontario. But if they think you're a cop, they won't say a word. I know those girls." She looked Bella directly in the eyes. "I used to be one of them. They don't trust cops and they're always looking for the customer that will give them a way out."

Bella turned to a fresh page in her notebook. "Can you give me names, descriptions of some of her friends?" Otherwise finding them would be like searching for a needle in a haystack. Bella needed a starting place.

Mrs. Maynard got up, taking her portable oxygen supplier with her, and went to the table where the television sat. She picked up a framed photograph and brought it to Bella. "She printed that from a picture she took with her phone. She said that way I know who her friends really are." She pointed to the redhead in the photo. "That's Jasmine. The brunette is Talia and the other blonde is Miranda. They've been friends for a good long while now. They're the best chance you've got at getting the truth."

"Thank you, Mrs. Maynard." Bella snapped a pic of the photo with her cell and then stood.

Pierce followed her lead. "We'll do all we can to find her," she assured the lady.

As they left, Bella warned Mrs. Maynard to keep her doors and windows locked and her phone close. She urged the woman not to allow anyone inside unless he or she showed proper credentials. Audrey likely didn't realize she'd put her mother in a perilous position as well. Sometimes people just didn't think.

Once she and Pierce were in her car, Pierce asked, "What now?"

"Now we find her friends and see if they'll talk to us." Bella thought about that for a moment. "Actually, I'm reasonably certain they would talk to you before they would me."

He stared at her. She kept her attention on the street but she could feel that blue gaze boring a hole into her.

"Whatever's necessary."

Bella glanced at him. He stared forward. If the man had a so-called red room, he shouldn't have any trouble approaching and charming a few ladies of the night.

The drive to Audrey Maynard's territory took just over twenty minutes. It didn't take long to spot the blonde and the redhead. Bella pulled to the curb on the opposite side of the street from the ladies.

She looked to her passenger. "Good luck."

He stared at her for a long moment and then got out. Bella watched as he closed the center button on his elegant suit, then squared his shoulders and strode across the street. The two women immediately started to smile and wave at him.

Bella couldn't hear the conversation but she could easily imagine how it was going down just watching the back-and-forth. The redhead, Jasmine, hugged his arm and leaned in close. He stared down at her upturned face for a moment and a spear of something hot cut through Bella.

Not jealousy, she told herself.

She shook it off and watched as he spoke, smiled and allowed the women to hang on him like he was Santa and they had waited all year for a chance to tell him what they wanted for Christmas. The blonde, Miranda, trailed her fingers up his back and into his silky hair. Bella had to look away for a moment.

"Don't be ridiculous," she muttered. Shaking her head, she forced her attention back across the street. The longer the women stroked him and leaned into him, the more uncomfortable she grew. She squirmed in her seat, her fingers tightening on the steering wheel.

Finally, when Pierce broke from the two, she was able to draw in a breath.

He returned to the car and settled into the passenger seat.

"Did you learn anything?" Her voice sounded too high to her own ears.

Pierce turned to her. He frowned. "What's wrong?"

Bella started to ask what he meant but then she caught a glimpse of herself in the rearview mirror. Her face was flushed.

"I'm fine. Did you find out where Audrey might be?"

Before he answered, he reached into his pocket and retrieved his cell. He glanced at the screen, touched the accept-call button and said, "Pierce."

Bella struggled to gather her composure while he listened to his caller. She relaxed her shoulders, took three deep breaths and loosened her grip on the steering wheel. Being so attracted to her client that she couldn't focus on the task at hand wouldn't do. It was out of character for her, and she didn't intend to let it become a part of her character now—no matter how ridiculously alluring Devon Pierce was.

Pierce thanked the caller and put his phone away. He turned to Bella. "That was Detective Corwin."

Bella braced for bad news. She did not want to hear that Audrey Maynard was dead. She thought of the worried mother they'd just visited who had likely introduced her daughter to the life.

"Have they found her?" She held her breath.

Pierce gave his head a shake. "No. But they did find a mechanic from the Lexus dealership. He'd been shot with a .32. Apparently the blood in the trunk of the stolen car was his. I'm guessing he was their way into the dealership for the vehicle."

Dread trickled through her. "Please tell me you don't own a .32."

"I don't."

Thank God. Bella started the car. Whether Pierce realized it or not, they were in trouble. The case just went from potential kidnapping and sexual abuse to murder.

And Dr. Devon Pierce was the only real person of interest.

Before heading to his home, they stopped by the hotel where Audrey Maynard had said she met with the man who hired her. The hotel refused to give out any information or to share security video footage without a warrant.

Maybe the police would have better luck.

Chapter Five

Arbor Drive, Lake Bluff, 7:48 p.m.

When they arrived at his home, Devon would have preferred to go inside alone. To have peace and quiet in which to consider the moving parts of this nightmare until he could put the pieces together and come up with some sort of logic.

If Richard was behind this insanity, and he must be, why now? Why involve Cara?

The answer echoed inside him. Because Richard understood. He knew without doubt that resurrecting the circumstances around his late wife's death was the only way to truly do harm to Devon. The nasty rumors of murder had died down not long after the funeral. But that didn't mean stirring them up wouldn't damage his reputation—and his industry-changing work at the Edge.

Ms. Lytle parked between the fountain and the front door. She shut off the engine and turned to him. "We need to talk and I expect total honesty."

He met her gaze in the fading car interior lights. "We haven't talked enough?"

His brain needed to shut down. He wasn't sure he could trust himself to make proper decisions or to hold a civil discourse at this point. To bring *this* here—to bring *her* here again—was too much.

"I don't think you fully grasp the weight of the situation. Someone is framing you and they're doing a hell of a good job. It's imperative that we stay ahead of this. By morning, the police could show up with a warrant. It's only logical that reporters will follow. We need to be prepared."

"Very well." He reached for the door. "We'll talk."

He'd wanted to return to the Edge to pick up his car but she'd insisted that she would be chauffeuring him everywhere until this nightmare was over. He thought the suggestion was ludicrous and yet here they were. He had other vehicles at his disposal. If he decided to dismiss her, other transportation was not an issue.

He trudged up the steps and to the front door. A few seconds later, they were inside. He locked the door behind them and reset the alarm out of habit. "Would you like a drink?"

Devon intended to have several. He rarely allowed himself more than one but tonight was different. Tonight he needed...*more*.

"No, thank you." She hesitated a moment then added, "You should eat first."

She stood several feet away and still she felt too close. A few strands of her dark hair had come loose and fallen around her face, softening her all-business appearance.

"My kitchen is at your disposal if you're hungry." The craving roaring inside him right now would not be satisfied with anything in that kitchen.

He made it to the bar and had reached for the bottle of Scotch he reserved for celebrations. This was certainly no celebration but he didn't care. He downed a substantial serving of the smoky, dry whiskey. Then he closed his eyes and willed himself to relax.

"What's on the page you stuffed into your pocket besides blood?"

He reluctantly opened his eyes and met her impatient stare. "It's a page from my late wife's private journal."

She looked surprised. No more so than he.

"How did someone get their hands on a page from her journal?"

He poured himself another drink. "That is an answer I would sincerely like to know myself."

He lifted the glass to his lips but her hand on his arm stopped him from turning up the bottom as he'd intended.

"I need your head on straight for the rest of the questions I have."

He stared at her for a moment, the glass mere centimeters from his mouth, her fingers somehow searing his skin through his clothing. "Trust me, Ms. Lytle, this is merely a bracer." He searched her dark eyes. "In fact, I'm certain you will prefer me without the fierce edge I'm experiencing at the moment."

Her hand fell away. He downed the drink.

When he'd savored the promised relief for a moment, he set the glass aside and turned to her. "Ask what you will. I'm all yours."

Had the last part been a Freudian slip? She stared at him as if she wondered the same.

"We can talk while we eat," she announced before turning and walking away.

He watched the determined strides, the sway of her hips, her back as straight as a ballerina's. That she had entered his private world troubled him immensely. This—he looked around the room—small sliver of his existence was intensely personal. The rest of his world was work. At work, he was in control, untouchable, respected. Here he was alone, desperate, needy. He kept the two worlds completely separate.

Isabella Lytle did not belong in this part.

He licked the lingering taste of Scotch from his lips. He couldn't deny his attraction to her. The challenge she represented intrigued him. Never had he seen a woman handle herself the way Bella Lytle did. She wasn't easily intimidated and her mind was quicksilver sharp. A part of him desired to throw caution to the wind and discover the woman underneath that professional facade. But no matter how much he craved her...no matter how much he wanted to take her completely apart, that would be a mistake.

He was well aware why he was suddenly so fascinated by this woman he hardly knew. The hunger for a physical outlet kept his mind away from the ugly past that had abruptly come back to haunt him.

In no hurry, he moved toward the kitchen. As he neared, he heard cabinet doors closing, dinnerware settling onto stone. When he entered the room, she stood at the open door of the refrigerator browsing the shelves. His house manager ensured the kitchen was stocked, providing numerous options. Usually he prepared dinner for himself each night, though recently he'd had no appetite.

She didn't inquire as to what he wanted to eat. Instead she prepared two small plates with cheese, fruit and cold cuts. To occupy himself, he went to the pantry and grabbed a box of crackers. She took the box and arranged the crackers next to the rest and then passed a plate to him.

Another trip to the refrigerator and she returned with two bottles of water. He reached into a drawer and retrieved linen napkins. They sat at the island and ate in silence. He forced himself to chew and then swallow. She was right about the alcohol. She was right about the rest as well. By morning, the police would be at his doorstep. He had to prepare.

She wanted him to tell her everything…to open himself up to her.

He caught himself staring at her and looked away. Whatever questions she had, she should ask them. Anything would be better than his preoccupation with her lips sliding across the tines of the fork or resting against the mouth of the water bottle. His control was slipping away quickly and he loathed the desperation clawing at him.

Not since Cara had anyone got under his skin quite like the beautiful and elusive Ms. Lytle.

"You had questions?" His tone was sharper than he'd intended.

She dabbed the napkin to her lips, and he stared at the place she had touched. Her lips were far too lush, too deeply colored. He licked his own, the urge to taste hers building deep inside him.

"Your wife kept a journal. Was there a particular reason she kept a record of her feelings while you were married or was this something she'd always done?"

He tossed his napkin atop his plate. He'd forced himself to eat a few bites but he couldn't stomach any more. "We were married for five years. I had no idea she kept a journal until shortly before her death."

"You discovered it and didn't like what you found?"

Her dark eyes probed his, looking for signs of untruths. She was very, very good at spotting those. He'd recognized her intense stares for what they were: a silent interrogation. Underneath her scrutiny, he felt his desire for her rise.

He wasn't used to being unsettled by a woman—or anyone else, for that matter. And the sensation made him want to unsettle her back.

"That's correct."

"Was this around the time of the accident?"

"Of course." He gave his head a slight shake. "Would the story be even half as titillating had I not made the discovery on the precipice of such a tragedy?"

"This is not fiction, Dr. Pierce," she chastised.

"Certainly not." He looked away for a moment. "I found her journal the day before we left for Binghamton, New York, her hometown. It was too late to change our plans. Her family was expecting us." He shrugged. "I suppose I was still in denial."

"You fought about it?"

"We fought, yes." The voices from that evening whispered through his mind, her ranting at him at the top of her lungs. Tears streaming down her beautiful face. His deeper voice, simmering with rage and threats of an ugly divorce, of leaving her with nothing. She threw her perfume bottle at him. He'd dodged and the elegant glass had smashed against the hearth of the fireplace in their room.

"Did you threaten her in any way?"

There was the tiniest glimmer of sadness in her eyes now. Or perhaps it was sympathy. Of all the things she had to offer, her sympathy was not what he wanted.

"I never threatened my wife with anything other than a divorce."

She tilted her head and stared at him. "The journal contained something inflammatory enough to make you consider a divorce? Did you have a prenuptial agreement?"

"I had suspected she was having an affair

for some time. As I told you before, I hoped it would pass. But the journal made it clear that would not be the case." He exhaled a big breath. "And no, there was no prenuptial agreement."

Ms. Lytle slipped from her seat and took her plate to the sink. She folded her napkin and left it on the counter. While he did the same, she said, "Do you still have the journal?"

"Yes." He braced his hands on the counter, his back to her. He knew it was only a matter of time before she asked to see it.

He felt raw, exposed, and he hated it. He was unused to being tipped off center, which this investigation had done. He wanted to rage against the unfairness of it. Unfortunately, the only outlet he had was Bella Lytle, who was off-limits. A professional contact only.

So why was he drawn to her in such a primal way? Why did he want to unsettle the cool-headed investigator as he'd been unsettled?

"What secrets did you discover?"

"The journal intimately detailed the affair that had been going on for six months."

"With your partner?"

Devon faced her then. "I didn't believe so at the time. Though the entries in her journal were quite explicit, she never named her co-conspirator."

"Where is it?"

"I keep it in my bedside table."

Dismay claimed her face. "You're serious." It wasn't a question. She recognized the truth.

"It reminds me every day not to trust anyone with my deepest, darkest secrets."

She shook her head. "Please tell me you haven't read it a thousand times."

"Only once." He stared at his hands, fingers spread on the cool surface of the granite countertop. "When I found it, I read all the way through."

"Why punish yourself that way?"

He met her gaze, saw the disapproval there. "Because I deserved to be punished if all that she felt was true."

She looked away first. "What significance did the final entry have? The one someone left for you in the trunk of a stolen car with a pool of blood."

He reached into his pocket for the crumpled page. He slapped it down on the sleek countertop, the crimson smear on the page a shocking contrast to the cool whites, browns and grays of the granite.

She picked up the page that had been torn loose from the rest. Part of the lower half had been left attached to the binding as if the page had been ripped away in a rush. Ms. Lytle didn't have to recite the words aloud. Devon knew them by heart.

He will kill me rather than risk anyone knowing the truth.

When her gaze rested on his once more, she asked, "What made her believe you would rather see her dead than to allow the truth to be told?"

He shook his head. "I have no idea. I asked what the hell she meant and her only response was that I didn't understand. She said I could never understand. That everything wasn't about me."

Apparently, his wife had been right. The final months of their marriage may not have been about him at all. Didn't mean he wasn't still left to pick up the pieces.

"What truth is she referring to?"

Devon gave the only answer he could. "I have no idea."

Whether she believed him or not, he couldn't say. She shrugged, stared at the page. "We should put this in a bag. Any prints or other evidence left behind are likely contaminated already, but we should preserve whatever possible." Her gaze settled onto his. "I'd like to see the journal."

There it was. Another breach of his carefully constructed existence.

His first instinct was to refuse her request. What difference could the autobiography of his wife's infidelity make now? But he understood that he was too close to this to see things clearly. Perhaps he couldn't see how beyond proving motive the journal might serve the investigation.

"Very well. I'll get it for you."

"I should have a look around your home as well." She glanced across the kitchen. "If there is anything else incriminating that the police might find when they execute their search, I need to see it first."

RATHER THAN ANSWER, Pierce only regarded her for one long moment. He wanted to deny her request; Bella could see that certainty in his eyes. Self-preservation, she suspected, kept him from doing so.

She was prepared to remind him of the agency's strict confidentiality policy and stellar investigator-client reputation when he said, "We'll take the grand tour, then."

Bella followed him through the first-floor rooms. A dining table that seated eighteen spanned the eclectic European dining room. Two powder rooms and a smoking room. The double doors she'd first noticed at the other end of the entry hall did lead to his study. The walls, bookshelves and desk were a rich mahogany. The shelves were lined with medical journals. Framed awards and achievements filled one wall. There were no photos of family. His parents were deceased and he had no other close relatives, according to the background material provided by the agency and her research.

She surveyed the lovely artwork on the walls as they climbed the east staircase. One by one, he showed her through the upper-floor wings of the house. So far she'd counted nine bedrooms, twelve baths and eighteen fireplaces. Every room was exquisitely decorated and utterly *empty* of any sign of a human touch beyond the decor.

From the windows that faced the back of the property, she saw the lights playing on Lake Michigan. She wondered if he and his wife had ever considered filling this home with children, or if it had only been a showplace to impress friends and associates. As far as Bella could see, it had become nothing more than a mausoleum. A large empty hotel where he spent his nights.

His suite was the last one they entered. The room was large, the decor at once elegant and comfortable. He walked to his side of the enormous bed and reached into the second drawer of his night table. The leather-bound journal wasn't large, about six by nine inches. He handed it to her.

"Have you always kept it here, in your bedroom?"

"Yes." He glanced around the room as if looking for somewhere to settle his attention.

"When did you notice the page missing?"

"I didn't know it was missing until we found it in the trunk of that car."

Bella measured the weight of the book. It weighed hardly anything and yet it had destroyed a marriage. "When is the last time you recall opening it?"

"The one and only time I've opened it. The day before we left for New York."

She left him standing near the bed as she walked through the closet. There were two actually. One on either side of the massive bath. The white closet was empty. Not even a speck of dust littered the shelves. He'd had all her things removed. The mahogany closet was filled with expensive suits and shoes. Ties were folded and displayed in glass cases. Neatly pressed shirts in dozens of colors hung in well-ordered rows. The room smelled of leather and that expensive cologne he wore.

She returned to the bedroom. He waited at the door, his tall frame blocking her exit from the closet.

"Have you seen all you need to see?"

Did he really expect her to forget what Detective Corwin had said? "I need to see *everything*. The room Corwin mentioned is not exempt. I suspect it will be named specifically in the warrant."

"As you wish."

This time, they descended the west-side staircase. He led the way along the back downstairs hall where the laundry room and mudroom were located. A door halfway between the two opened onto a small landing. A less ornate staircase descended into the basement level, though nothing about the space looked like a basement.

The stairs ended in a large game room. A pool table stood in the center. A bar wrapped around one corner of the space. The biggest television she'd ever seen in her life hung on one wall. The wraparound seating area created the perfect conversation spot. Another fireplace. Another bathroom.

And a final door.

He took his wallet from his trousers and removed a key from its hiding place. He opened the door and pushed it inward, then turned on the lights.

The first thing she noticed was the seemingly endless amount of black. The walls were black; the floor and ceiling were black. All appeared to be leather. A bed—or something in the shape of a bed—was the single red element, also leather. She moved around the room. A row of shelves displayed an abundance of sex toys, whips and the like, some objects not readily identifiable. Every imaginable kind of condom filled a glass fishbowl.

Her heart started to pound harder and harder. A refreshment center claimed a few feet against the wall. The glass door of the fridge revealed wine coolers, beer, colas and bottled water. Opposite the bed, a steel bar hung horizontally, maybe eight feet from the floor. Chains hung from the bar. Padded handcuffs dangled on the ends of the chains.

Before she could stop her runaway imagination, she pictured Devon Pierce shackled there. Naked, of course. His lean body taut in expectation of the whip's sting. Her nipples hardened and an ache throbbed between her thighs.

She should not be here.

He waited at the door, watching her, assessing her reaction.

Could he see how aroused she was?

She turned on him. "Do you bring women here regularly?"

"How is that relevant, Ms. Lytle?"

"Ms. Maynard accused you of holding her

here. For two months. Can anyone else refute that accusation? Someone you brought here for an evening of entertainment in the past few weeks?" Even as she asked the questions, her throat grew so dry she could hardly speak. Her pulse was racing. Her skin was on fire.

She needed out of this room.

"I haven't brought anyone here recently." He took a step in her direction. "Perhaps a month ago." Another couple of feet disappeared between them.

"That would be within the two-month time frame. Do you have contact information for her? She may be needed as a witness if Mrs. Maynard's testimony about Audrey's whereabouts doesn't suffice."

"The sorts of women I bring here don't provide contact information."

He was standing right next to her now, staring down at her as if she were his partner for the evening.

"You shouldn't be afraid of your desire, Isabella," he said in a low voice that made her wonder what he saw in her expression.

She blinked. "Bella," she corrected. "My friends call me Bella."

"Bella." He licked his lips when he said her name as if tasting it. "It suits you."

She said nothing. She couldn't. Her skin was flushed. Her state of agitation was obvious.

He reached up, traced a finger along her cheek. She shivered. "You are very beautiful, Bella."

"Is that what you tell them when you bring them here?" A flash of anger melted into anticipation. "Every woman wants to be called beautiful. Is that what you do for the women you bring home? Make them feel special, wanted, sexy?"

His hand flattened on her chest, the tips of his fingers tracing the collar of her blouse. Her body throbbed at his firm touch.

His fingers trailed more softly against the hollow of her throat. "Is that how you feel, Bella? Special? Sexy?"

She tried not to shiver but his words, the sound of his voice, made her ache with want. "Maybe a little."

His hand moved lower, slipping inside her jacket, closing around her breast. Her breath caught. He squeezed. Pleasure shot through her.

She lifted her chin in defiance of her own weakness. "I should go."

He moved in closer. The fingers of his left hand closed around the nape of her neck, threaded into her hair, loosening the pins holding it. His right hand squeezed her breast harder then slid down to her waist and slid around to the small of her back. He pulled her against his body. She felt every hard ridge and angle of him.

Slowly, so very slowly, he lowered his face to hers. Their lips brushed. She gasped. Sought someplace for her hands. No. No. She couldn't touch him... If she touched him now, the battle would be over.

As if he'd abruptly realized his mistake, he stepped away from her. She swayed, struggled to regain her equilibrium.

"You should stay here tonight. Her journal doesn't leave this house. Choose whatever guest room you like."

Were his attempts to put her off balance some endeavor to push her away from this ultra-personal part of the investigation? Did he somehow believe he could prevent her from dissecting this facet of his history? No way. In fact, it was her turn to put him off balance.

"I'll take this room."

He hesitated at the door but didn't look back. Oh yes, direct hit. When he'd gone, she removed her jacket and folded it like a pillow on the enormous red leather bed. She toed off her shoes and relaxed onto the overly firm surface. She opened the journal of Cara Pierce and started to read.

An hour and many pages later, she came to the first entry that changed dramatically in tone.

I shouldn't have allowed myself to be seduced. Or perhaps I was the one doing the seducing. We were both equally surprised. We spent hours together, never leaving the rumpled sheets of the bed. My adventurous lover learned every part of me. Every secret place that longed for more than I ever hoped for. This was the most sexually demanding and beautiful encounter of my life.

I want more.

Bella closed the journal and laid it aside. She stood and walked around the room. She paused at the shelves and studied the various bondage items. Ropes, handcuffs, collars. She fingered a leather riding crop. Blindfolds, vibrators, clamps. She moved to the steel bar at the other end of the room. The chains and padded cuffs dangling from the bar again had her imagining Pierce restrained there. Would he want his playmate to use that riding crop to torture him or would she be on her knees in front of him?

Need pulsed deep inside her. Though Cara Pierce clearly had not been speaking of her husband in that journal passage, Bella had imagined him doing those things to her. Her hand went to her breast, to the one he had squeezed so tightly. Her nipples remained as hard as stone.

She wasn't a prude. She'd played a few sex games, but nothing on this level.

It was late. She should get some sleep. She lay down on the red leather bed once more. She stared at the ceiling, only then noticing the mirror. She touched her breast again, thought of his hand there and then sliding lower. She closed her eyes and thought of him kissing every part of her, exploring every hot, shivery inch. Bringing her to release over and over with nothing more than his skilled hands and those incredible lips. She rolled onto her side and bit down on her lower lip to hold back her cries when desire rippled through her.

She drifted off to sleep while images of him spooned against her, kissing her all over, followed her into her dreams.

Chapter Six

Wednesday, June 6, 6:05 a.m.

He was trying to distract her.

Bella finger-combed her hair, then arranged it into her preferred twist and pinned it into place. She smoothed her sweater and slipped into her jacket. He distracted her because he didn't want to answer those hard, personal questions.

She stepped back into the room with its massive red leather bed. She was glad the space had included an en suite bath. Though the stainless-steel garden tub had given her pause, she supposed it was as much a design statement as a place to indulge in sexual activity.

She stared at the red leather bed as she exited the bath. Before she could stem the flow, a stream of images—all involving Devon Pierce naked—filled her mind. With a shake of her head, she opened the journal and read through a few more entries. Cara was meeting her lover at least once a week, most often twice. The interludes were intensely erotic.

My lover flogged me today. It was my first experience with sexual torture. No one has ever touched me that way. I was secured facedown on the bed with my arms and legs spread wide. The whip didn't break the skin but created red welts everywhere it touched. I cried out, the tears stinging my eyes as the leather stung my skin. Then my lover licked and kissed every red mark on my body, soothing and suckling until I was dizzy with desire. I don't dare write of the other things. All I can say is that I have never experienced a full body orgasm until today. It went on and on and I can't get enough.

Bella shivered as she closed the journal and tucked it into her bag. No matter how much Devon Pierce wanted to believe a warrant wasn't coming, Bella knew better. It was a matter of time before the cavalry came calling. For that reason, despite his edict that the journal was not to leave the house, it was going with her.

She fingered the inflammatory volume in her bag while she considered the ramifications of withholding evidence, but decided that this wasn't exactly evidence—not for Audrey Maynard's allegations of kidnapping, anyway, which was what the cops were investigating. The police did not need to know about the journal. The affair Cara Pierce was involved in would prove motive for her husband for a death that had already been investigated and deemed an accident. At this point, there was no need to stir up trouble on that front. Having it turned into a murder investigation all these years later wouldn't help anyone.

Speaking of Dr. Pierce, Bella found him in the kitchen pouring himself a coffee. He wore a navy suit today with an equally dark blue shirt, the fabric no doubt the finest available, like the rest of his wardrobe. The jacket hung on the back of a chair at the small breakfast table perched in the large bay window. She placed her bag on the floor next to a stool that stood at the counter. The decision not to bring up last night's incident was an easy one to make.

"Good morning." She reached for a mug.

He shifted his attention to her, the French-press carafe in his hand. "Good morning." He filled her cup without her having to ask. "I won't inquire as to how you slept. That room was not designed for comfort."

"Surprisingly well." She inhaled deeply of the bold flavored coffee. Whether it was the blend or the French press, it smelled incredible. She tasted it and moaned before she could stop herself. "You're very good with coffee, Dr. Pierce."

"I'm very good with many things, Ms. Lytle."

She studied his handsome face. She knew this whole investigation was torture for him. A man so private suddenly forced to reveal his deepest desires wasn't going to handle it with grace. He was going to deflect and strike out. He knew he had got to her last night and he hoped to use his new discovery to keep her off balance. Not happening. "I'm confident you are. I thought we had dispensed with the formalities. Call me Bella."

"Bella." He said her name as if tasting wine and attempting to dissect the flavor.

"After my grandmother." She sipped the delicious coffee and shifted her focus to the news on the television across the room. "I hope I haven't caused you to be late this morning." He'd told her that his usual workday began around seven.

"I sometimes work from my office here." He set his cup aside.

She really needed to go by her place and pick up a change of clothes. The shower had been refreshing but her clothes were heavy with yesterday's tension.

"Did the journal provide any insights that might help you solve the case?"

The question was one he genuinely wanted an answer to, she knew this, but the tone of his question was caustic, indifferent. He wanted to appear uncaring, but the good doctor was not quite as adept at lying about this particular subject as he would obviously prefer her to believe.

"Not yet. I have a ways to go."

The tension along his jawline warned that he was not pleased with her reading those so very private entries.

"Your wife must have been a very selfish woman."

Bella had done her research. Rather than spend some of her time and efforts to charitable pursuits, Cara Pierce traveled extensively while her husband devoted himself entirely to his work. She wore extravagant clothes and jewelry and she refused to have children. That was something Bella had learned in the journal. Pierce—Devon—wanted children. His wife adamantly did not. She bemoaned the idea of ruining her body with stretch marks.

How had he fallen in love with a woman who held so little in common with him?

"She traveled all the time while you worked," she added for clarification.

"Perhaps she was merely lonely. I was not a very attentive husband."

The doorbell rang before she could argue with his reasoning.

Devon picked up a remote and changed the channel on the small television mounted near the refrigerator. The image on the screen was of his front door and the parking enclave. Several cars besides her own sat around the center fountain. Detectives Corwin and Hodge stood at the door, a couple of uniforms and what looked like a crime scene team behind them.

"So it begins," Pierce muttered.

Bella set her cup aside and followed him through the house. "Where's your housekeeper?"

"My house manager and her staff have the week off."

"You gave everyone the same week off?" she asked as they walked across the glossy marble and headed for the door.

"She oversees the cleaning staff and the landscaping team. It's best that they vacation at the same time."

She got it now. If the rest of the staff was off at the same time as the manager, he didn't have to interact with them.

They reached the door just as another chime of the bell echoed through the vast hall. "I'll handle this," she said, hoping he would acquiesce to her offer.

He gestured to the door and stepped back. She understood how detectives analyzed their persons of interest. Corwin and Hodge would be scrutinizing his every word, his every look. They made it their mission to understand how to get under his skin. How to prod responses. Pierce would be far better served to not give them any more ammunition.

Bella opened the door and flashed the detectives a smile. "Good morning, gentlemen." She opened the door wide as she stepped back. "Please come in."

Corwin thrust the warrant at Pierce without bothering to say good morning or even hello. From the dark circles under his eyes and the rumpled suit, he'd likely been working all night. Bella remembered well the necessary hours required to investigate a case like this one. No one wanted more bodies piling up.

One of the uniforms stayed outside the door while the other came inside. The team of forensic techs spilled in next. Hodge hooked a thumb toward them. "They'll be here for a while."

Bella nodded. "As long as nothing is damaged and every single thing they touch is put back exactly as it was, you won't get any trouble from us."

Corwin strolled over to her, close enough to

whisper his question. "Isn't that the same suit you were wearing yesterday?"

Bella looked him up and down, and when she responded, she didn't whisper. "That's funny— I was just thinking the same thing about those khaki trousers and the tweed jacket you're wearing. With the white shirt it's a little more difficult to say, but there is the matter of all those wrinkles."

The other detective's lips quirked with the need to smile.

Moving on to business, Bella filled in the two detectives as to what Maynard's mother had to say, including the part about her daughter being home recently. If she'd been held hostage by Pierce for the past two months as she'd claimed, it was unlikely that he'd allow her to go home for visits.

"Any news on Audrey Maynard's whereabouts?" Pierce asked, his tone sharp, impatient.

Hodge shrugged. "Nothing. It's like she dropped off the planet."

"Or got dead," Corwin countered. He looked from Bella to Pierce and back. "I'm presuming the two of you were together last night."

"That's correct," Bella said without hesitation. "We worked late. Rather than drive an hour home, it was more reasonable that I stay here."

The techs fanned out, taking the upstairs rooms first. Corwin shifted his attention to Pierce. The doctor was six or more inches taller than either of the detectives, so looking up was necessary. "Hodge and I would like to see the red room."

"I think you've watched too many movies, gentlemen." Pierce indicated they should follow him. "What I have is an adult game room."

Bella suspected the room wasn't about games or even sexual pleasure; the space was about punishment. She kept those thoughts to herself. Who was she to cast the first stone? God knew she had plenty of her own hang-ups.

En route, Bella gathered her bag. She didn't want one of the techs poking into her things, particularly the journal. Cara Pierce's private notes about her life were not something these guys needed to see just yet. Not until Bella had something to neutralize the advantage the glaring motive the woman's words appeared to provide.

While Corwin and Hodge were examining the numerous sex toys, Bella pulled Pierce aside and warned him that this could take all day, maybe longer. If he wanted her to stay and go through the house with the detectives, she would gladly do so. At this point, however, her instincts were leaning toward sticking to him.

So far, the trouble that had shown up at his doorstep was designed to create issues for him, but that scenario could change quickly. If the person behind this obvious setup felt his ultimate goal was not being accomplished quickly enough, he could make an attempt on Pierce's life. At least one person had lost his life so far.

Pierce apparently felt the same. He called in the house manager's chief assistant to stay with the house while the police did what they had to do. During the drive into the city, Bella had a captive audience for a little more than an hour. She decided now was as good a time as any to bring up her concerns about his private staff.

"I'm sure you vet your staff very carefully," she began, "but your wife's journal was kept in your bedside table. There was a page torn from it. I have to say that it's very likely you have an employee who is willing to take money in exchange for access to your home, or at least to the things inside your home."

"I am aware that scenario is swiftly becoming one I cannot deny." His voice was grim. "My security system is not one easily breached. If the system had been tampered with, audio or video altered, I would know it. The page was either given to my former partner, or he was allowed into my home after the security system had been turned off."

Bella merged onto the interstate. "You're convinced, then, that it's Sutter."

"I can think of no one else who knew me well enough to know my weaknesses. Jack Hayman never showed any interest in my personal life. Even now, he spends most of his time on a beach somewhere surrounded by exotic women. I doubt he would go to all this trouble for any reason."

If Hayman was ruled out and it was Sutter who had the affair with Pierce's wife, he likely knew all his secrets. Cara would have shared plenty with her lover.

"Did you have the adult game room before she died?" Traffic was already crazy heavy. Those who lived in the suburbs were winding their way into the city, their automobiles lined up bumper to bumper.

"No. That came after."

She thought of the things his late wife had said in her journal. Clearly her secret lover was playing those same sorts of games with her. "Were you and your wife intimate in that way?"

"Are you asking me if we played games? Used pleasure enhancements?"

Heat flushed her skin, making her want to squirm in her seat. She was a professional investigator who'd asked any number of personal questions throughout her career. She'd heard it all, from all kinds of people. It took a hell of a lot more than sexual kink to knock her off balance.

And yet that was exactly what Dr. Devon Pierce and his ridiculously sexy adult game room had done.

As uncomfortable as asking made her, she needed to know—to understand the dynamics between them. Didn't she?

"Did you?"

"No. I was very busy and preoccupied. I'm certain she considered our sex life quite boring."

After the way he'd touched Bella last night, she doubted sex with Pierce would be boring by any definition of the word. "You were married for five years before the accident. Surely there was a time when the two of you were happy."

The silence was so thick it was difficult to breathe. She adjusted her grip on the steering wheel, stared at the rows of taillights in front of her. The decision to have this conversation now suddenly felt incredibly awkward. Pretending that last night hadn't happened felt like the right thing to do when she'd got up this morning. In spite of that decision, there was no way around talking about sex.

"We were happy at first. She became jealous of my work. Felt neglected. Rightfully so." He sighed and stared out the window. "I'm not sure anything I could have done differently would have mattered, but I will always wonder."

Bella allowed the silence to settle between them.

They'd just taken the exit for downtown when he answered a call on his cell. "I'm almost there," he said to the caller. When he'd put his phone away, he surveyed the traffic. "A bus loaded with children headed to a dance competition crashed on the expressway. Most of the injured are en route to the Edge."

Even as he said the words, a half dozen ambulances seemed to appear out of nowhere, sirens blaring.

By the time they reached the parking area, the ambulances were already lined up at the emergency entrance. Bella pulled as close to the area as possible. "Go," she said. "I'll park and catch up with you inside."

She watched until Pierce was safely inside. She parked her car and hurried to the ER's entrance. Gurneys were rushing in with patients while others were rushing out to retrieve more. Children were wailing. Mothers were crying. Keeping her attention on their faces rather than their bloody bodies, Bella hurried to the registration desk.

"What can I do to help?"

The two registration specialists glanced at her. The older of the two evidently recognized her as a friend of Dr. Pierce's.

"We've got six adults, including the bus driver, here who were with the children," said the older woman, Patsy, according to her name tag. "But we'll have a whole lot more showing up. There're sixteen children. The parents of the others will be arriving any minute. If you can keep them calm until we get the paperwork done, that would be great."

Bella nodded. "I can do that."

As Patsy said, a dozen or more cars descended on the ER parking lot in the half hour that followed. Frantic parents were not easily placated. One of the mothers who had been on the bus and who was uninjured helped with passing along information about whose child was where. Some were at imaging; others were in treatment rooms. Thankfully only two had injuries serious enough to warrant surgery.

One by one, the parents were reunited with their children in treatment rooms or in the ER lobby if they had been released.

When everyone appeared settled, Bella walked through the double doors into the corridor beyond the triage area. She passed the nurses' station. As she approached Treatment Room Six, she heard Pierce's voice.

The door opened and a nurse walked out. She smiled at Bella and left the door partially open. A girl—six or seven years old, Bella guessed—sat on the exam table. Her left eye was swollen and swiftly turning colors. There was a bandage on her right leg. The mother stood on the opposite side of her, her worried face showing her struggle to keep up with what Pierce was saying.

"Bethany is going to be fine, but the images show a small linear skull fracture."

The mother covered her mouth with her hands. "Oh my God." Tears flowed down her cheeks.

"There's no shift or movement in the bones—that's a very good thing. Most likely we can simply monitor her overnight and send her home."

The mother's hands came away from her mouth, rested at her throat. "So she'll be okay."

"Absolutely. But," he said carefully, "because I'm not one to take chances with the life of such a precious little girl—" he smiled down at the child "—we're going to transfer her over to Rush Medical Center for the night. The nurse is taking care of the arrangements now."

The worry was back. The mother's face paled. "Something is wrong."

The little girl looked from her mother to Pierce and back. "Mommy?"

"This is just to make me feel better, Mrs. Jamison, I assure you. If on the outside chance Bethany needs any additional treatment, she will be in the best hospital this city has. I'm quite certain that's not going to happen, but I would feel better if she was there. I think you'll both rest better tonight at Rush."

"All right. My husband is on the way. Can we wait to be moved until he's here?"

"Of course." Pierce held out his hand to the little girl. She shook it with all her might. "You are a very brave little girl, Bethany. Your mother and father should be very proud."

The little girl grinned and the mother thanked him profusely. Before he could get away, she grabbed him and hugged him fiercely.

When at last the relieved mother released him, he walked out of the room. When he saw Bella, surprise flashed in his eyes. Bella smiled. "I had no idea you had such a way with children."

"I'm only an ogre with beautiful women."

Bella laughed. She had a feeling Dr. Devon Pierce was no monster at all. The problem was all those secrets he'd been keeping for so long. They tended to weigh a person down, darken their spirit. "You would make a very good father."

"No." He captured her eyes with his own, his gaze hard. "I wouldn't."

Stinging from his pointed rebuke, she shadowed him as he moved through the ER ensuring all was under control. Their next stop was in the surgery unit, where he checked on the two patients now in recovery. Both were doing well and would be moving on to Rush for admission.

As they walked toward his office, Bella paused and waited for him to meet her gaze. "It's time we tracked down your old partners and found out what they've been up to."

"If nothing else," he said, looking away, "you'll learn that my wife wasn't the only person who felt cheated by me."

As long as they learned which one felt cheated badly enough to seek revenge, Bella could deal with the rest. The sooner this case was solved, the less likely she was to cross the line she had brushed far too closely last night.

Chapter Seven

Chicago Police Department, 1:00 p.m.

Detective Corwin had called. He'd asked Devon to come downtown at his earliest convenience.

"They found something."

Bella's words reverberated inside him as she sent him a pointed glance before turning back to maneuvering through Chicago traffic. She'd insisted on driving. He'd agreed without protest. He wasn't entirely sure he could trust his ability to focus at this time. Not to mention his car was at home. The woman who'd pretended to be his wife remained missing, unless they had found her body and that was the reason for this command appearance.

"We really should call your attorney," she repeated. She'd made this statement twice already.

"I'll call my attorney if I need him."

Too many people were aware of his weaknesses and secrets already. He detested the idea that the woman driving had learned the most private part of him. His ability to experience pleasure came only with pain. He could only imagine how many more people would be involved before this was over.

"You holding up okay?"

If he didn't say something, she would continue prodding at him. "Why wouldn't I be? The police believe I'm a murderer, perhaps a repeat offender if Maynard is not found alive. I see no readily available avenue for refuting their insinuations."

He chose not to discuss the subject of how Ms. Lytle must see him. She was attracted to him; that was evident. As much as he would like to learn every part of her, he would be far more pleased if she respected his accomplishments. Whatever else he was beyond the creator of the Edge was of little value.

Hadn't his own wife proved as much? He was unable to please her…unable to make her happy in any way.

"You know, you could have stood by your position that they call your attorney with further questions."

"I might as well get it over with," he confessed. "Otherwise, they'll believe my lack of cooperation is yet further proof that I'm guilty."

He'd considered this at length during the long sleepless hours last night. He had nothing to hide—at least nothing related to criminal activity.

Bella parked on the street near their destination. "What they believe is irrelevant." She turned to face him. "All that matters is what they can prove."

They emerged from her sedan simultaneously. "What do you believe?"

She met his gaze over the car. "I believe someone is trying very hard to make you look guilty. Let's not give them any help."

She'd avoided his question. Perhaps her avoidance was an answer in itself.

Inside the precinct, they were escorted to a small conference room and offered water or soft drinks. He declined and she did as well. They didn't speak while they waited. Devon felt confident the detectives were listening in hopes of gleaning some tidbit that would support their case. Ten minutes, then fifteen passed. The delay was another tactic designed to make him restless, to heighten his anxiety.

Rather than allow their attempts to get under his skin to take root, he thought of all the children who'd been injured this morning and how exhilarated he'd felt caring for them.

He missed that part of his work. The patients.

Although his accomplishments were designed to ensure a higher patient survival rate in the ER setting, he couldn't deny missing the hands-on part of medicine. He thought of the volunteer work one of his nurses, Eva Bowman, did at a free clinic. Maybe he should consider an option such as that one.

His thoughts drifted from helping others to self-indulgence. Touching Bella hadn't been his plan last night. He'd reluctantly showed her what she wanted to see but then he saw her expression. She'd been affected, aroused—not repulsed as he would have imagined. Suddenly, he'd found himself lost in the smell of her, aching at the sight of her. The room was not for his pleasure and yet he'd taken great pleasure standing in the space and merely touching her.

For that he deserved to be punished severely.

When Corwin entered, Hodge came in right behind him. Both carried paper cups filled with steaming coffee from the corner shop. Now they were merely trying to make him angry. *Let's waste the doctor's time while we go for coffee.* Devon wasn't falling for it. The two detectives had unquestionably been observing their prey while someone else strolled to the corner coffee shop. Another game. Nothing more.

"We had to call out another team," Corwin

said as he sat down. "That's a big house you've got, Dr. Pierce."

Devon said nothing in response.

"Did you finish?" Bella demanded. "I certainly hope you left things the way you found them."

Hodge shrugged. "We do our best."

"Why are we here?" she demanded.

Corwin sipped his coffee, then leaned back in his chair. "I know I said this before, but I swear you act more like an attorney than an ex-cop. If I hadn't reviewed your record personally, I would have my doubts."

"You were a good cop," Hodge said.

"Are we going somewhere with this?" She looked from one to the other. "Dr. Pierce has a medical facility to oversee. A medical facility that's an integral part of this community. I'm certain there are people far higher up the food chain than the two of you who understand the importance of his work."

The two shared a look of feigned disbelief. "I guess we better get on with it," Corwin said.

"Yeah," Hodge agreed. "We wouldn't want the mayor or anyone important giving us any grief."

"You know," Corwin added, speaking to Bella, "you're only in here because the doctor insisted."

"Perhaps you'd rather deal with my attorney," Devon suggested.

Corwin shut his mouth on the subject. Still, he had that look. The one that said they had something. Whatever they had found, it was significant. The two were far too cocky to believe otherwise. Devon knew Bella had the journal, not that he was happy about her taking it out of his house. As it turned out, the move was a smart one. Anything else the police could have found was no doubt planted.

Bella was right about something else as well. He had a traitor on his staff. There was no way around that conclusion.

"First," Corwin began, "we found blood in the pocket of one of your suit jackets."

Hell. The journal page. Some of the blood on it must have still been transferable.

"You're aware we opened the trunk and found the blood," Devon offered.

"So you touched the blood?" Corwin argued.

"He's a doctor," Bella put in. "A physician's instinct would be to check to see where the blood was coming from and whether or not it was still warm and pliable."

Devon resisted the urge to stare at her. She hadn't lied, exactly, but she'd skirted all around it.

Corwin nodded. "You see, Hodge. I told you

he'd have an explanation for why the blood was in his pocket."

Hodge bobbed his head up and down. "He's smart. I'll give him that."

"Gentlemen," Bella said, interrupting their back-and-forth, "why don't we move on to why you asked Dr. Pierce here? Just this morning, there was a terrible bus crash on the expressway. I'm sure you heard about it. The Edge was inundated with the victims of that crash. Dr. Pierce doesn't have time for guessing games."

Bravo. Devon resisted the urge to smile.

"We found this." Corwin nodded and Hodge placed a large envelope on the table. Corwin removed the items inside. A woman's purse. A prescription bottle. A hairbrush sporting several blond hairs. And, finally, a strip of three photos—the kind from one of those photo booths one might see in a mall. All carefully packaged in clear plastic bags and labeled as evidence.

Devon didn't have to pick up the prescription bottle to know to whom it belonged. Images of Audrey Maynard stared at him from the photo strip.

"Audrey Maynard has never been in my home." Devon looked from Hodge to Corwin. "Until she showed up at the ER, I had never heard her name or met her."

"You're sticking by your story that this is a setup," Corwin offered, skepticism heavy in his tone.

"Detective," Bella countered, "do you really have to ask? Considering I was once a cop, you must know that I was well aware you would be coming with a warrant. Dr. Pierce and I had more than ample time to ensure nothing incriminating or inflammatory would be found at his home. Why would he leave a crucial piece of evidence for you to find? This entire situation is swiftly turning into a circus."

Corwin stared directly at Devon. "If you're being framed, Dr. Pierce, help us understand who would do such a thing. We're operating in the dark beyond what evidence you see and all of it points to you. If you're innocent, then give us a different direction to go in."

"We have no choice but to follow the evidence," Hodge reminded Bella. "Any cop knows that."

"Jack Hayman," Devon said, ignoring Bella's glance when he supplied the name. "He was my partner for several years. We parted under less-than-amicable terms. I can think of no one else who would go to these extents."

"What about a former patient?" Corwin asked. "Haven't you ever lost a patient or left one unsatisfied?"

"I've never left a patient unsatisfied, Detective." Devon reined in his frustration. "The only patient I've ever lost—"

"Was your wife," Corwin said for him. "Does your late wife have any family members who might feel you were responsible for her death? A brother? Father? Anyone?"

"Father, mother, a brother and two sisters," Devon said. "They still invite me to holiday gatherings. I doubt one of them has suddenly decided I did something wrong and somehow contributed to Cara's death."

Bella stared at him in surprise but she quickly recovered. "Is there anything else?" she asked the detectives. "If not, I see no reason for Dr. Pierce to be detained further. He has answered your questions and has nothing further to add."

"Maynard's mother confirmed her daughter was at home on several occasions the past few weeks, so her accusations against you do appear to be unfounded. But we're far from done with this, Dr. Pierce." Corwin stood. "We're turning this city upside down looking for Maynard. If we can find her alive, maybe she can shed some light on what's really going on. Meanwhile, we'll look up this Jack Hayman character, your former partner."

"Thank you." Devon glanced at the items on the table as he followed Bella from the room.

The likelihood that Maynard was still alive grew slimmer every day that she remained missing. It wasn't necessary to be a cop to recognize that sad statistic. The person who had planned this elaborate game had taken great care to perfectly cover all possibilities.

But perfection was an unattainable goal. There would be a mistake somewhere. All Devon had to do was find it.

They were in the car before Bella spoke. "You never mentioned that her family still contacts you."

"You didn't ask." He fastened his seat belt. "I didn't see how that information was relevant."

She eased the car into traffic. "As long as you're certain they're not holding you accountable for her death, then it's not."

"I'm certain."

"Why did you give them Hayman's name when it's more likely Sutter they should be trying to find?"

"Because I want to speak to Sutter first. I'm counting on you to recognize if he's lying."

She met his gaze for a second. "Where can we find him?"

"We'll start with his wife."

Mariah Sutter always seemed to have a soft spot for Devon, at least until Cara died. She distanced herself from him afterward. She could very well refuse to speak to him at all. He supposed it would depend upon how angry she was with Richard today. The two had a volatile relationship.

Perhaps if he told her that he suspected Richard of having an affair with Cara she would spill her guts. But then she would tell the police when they inevitably interviewed her.

Then they would have a motive that, to their way of thinking, had been festering for years.

Clark Street, 4:00 p.m.

SHOEHORNED BETWEEN FORMER industrial landmarks that were now stunning homes, the Sutter residence was a sleek Asian-inspired showplace. The outdoors was beautifully incorporated into the indoor living space, complete with a rooftop deck and unparalleled views of the city's skyline.

Bella decided that despite Sutter's failed partnership with Pierce, the man had done exceedingly well financially. The house alone had to be worth north of twelve million. She could only imagine the value of the artwork and the furnishings.

Why would a man with all *this* to lose risk carrying out a plot like the one plaguing Pierce? Was revenge for a professional and perhaps personal grievance several years in the past really worth such an enormous sacrifice?

Mariah Sutter breezed into the expansive entertaining area in a floor-length gauzy white covering that gave her an air of floating. The sheer fabric did little to conceal a minuscule gold bathing suit beneath. Sutter was fifty but her body looked like that of a twenty-year-old.

"Devon!" She held her hands out to him as she approached. "What a delight to see you."

He took her hands, leaned in and kissed her cheek. "The pleasure is always mine."

The older woman looked to Bella. "And who is this?" She beamed a smile at Devon. "Have you finally decided to stop living like a hermit?"

Bella blushed. She hated the reaction but she'd been cursed with the response since she was a child.

"Mariah Sutter, this is Isabella Lytle, my associate. We're working on a new project." He smiled at Bella and her blush deepened.

"Nice to meet you, Mrs. Sutter."

"Hmm. She's far too attractive for a mere associate. And so polite." Mariah sighed. "Please sit down and visit for a while. It's been ages. Would you like a refreshment?"

"Water would be nice," Bella said when Mariah's gaze rested on her.

"The same for me."

The words had no more been uttered than a man wearing only a tight-fitting swimsuit walked in carrying a tray of glasses filled with ice water and decorated with wedges of lime.

When they had been served, he left the room, his gaze lingering on Mariah as he walked away.

"The proverbial pool boy," she said with a laugh. "I do adore surrounding myself with attractive humans."

"Mariah," Devon said, "I would like a meeting with Richard. Is he in town?"

"He's in Wimbledon. He has a niece who's playing. He wanted me to go but, frankly, I can't tolerate the girl's mother. She is such a pretentious bitch."

"How long has he been in the London area?"

Bella let Devon handle the questions this time. Anything she asked would no doubt be viewed as suspicious.

Mariah appeared to consider the question. "A week now, I think. He won't return for another two. I'm sure he'll pop over to Wentworth for a few rounds of golf. You know Richard—he likes to take advantage of every opportunity to put something in a hole."

Bella felt another blush climbing her throat.

Mariah laughed. "I do believe I've embarrassed your associate, Devon."

Bella smiled. "Not at all. Are you a golfer as well?"

"Good heavens, no. I prefer shopping." Her gaze lingered on Bella. "For all sorts of beautiful things."

Bella had the distinct impression the older woman was flirting with her.

"If you would," Devon said, drawing Mariah's attention to him, "let Richard know I need a conference call. Nothing too time-consuming. Only a few minutes of his time."

"I hope he hasn't filed another of those ridiculous lawsuits." She rolled her eyes. "The man is admittedly a very bad sport. I say let bygones be bygones. I never liked losing a good friend over something as trivial as money."

"I noticed the Lexus in your courtyard," Bella said. "I've considered trying one. Have you been pleased with yours?"

"I have no complaints. Really, transportation is Richard's department. He brings them home and I drive them."

"I suppose the dealership has a good service department." Bella watched the other woman closely as she waited for an answer.

"We have someone who picks the vehicles up

when they need servicing. They always bring a replacement. Like clockwork."

Bella made a decision. She reached for her cell and pulled up the picture of Audrey Maynard. "Have you ever met this woman?"

Mariah reached for a pair of cheaters on the table next to her chair. She slipped on the narrow gold frames and peered at the photo.

"Oh yes. I think she's one of Richard's assistants. Or at least, that's what he called her. My guess is she was one of his flings. He does so love the young things." Mariah frowned and then looked to Devon. "I never noticed how much she looks like Cara." She turned back to Bella. "Why do you ask? Is she involved with something my husband should know about?"

"She may be," Devon said. "She's missing and the police are searching for her."

"The police? Whatever for?"

"A number of charges," Bella said before he could. "It's imperative we find her."

"When I can get in touch with Richard, I'll let him know."

"Mariah, has Richard spoken recently about seeking revenge against me? As much as I appreciate your graciousness today, we both know Richard despises me."

"You think Richard has something to do with whatever she's doing."

"I think someone is trying to make me believe that," he allowed. "If that's the case, Richard may be vulnerable as well."

"I wish I could say Richard would never do such a thing, but I can't." Mariah shook her head. "He isn't the same since the two of you ended your partnership. The cancer only made him more bitter. I don't know him anymore, and in truth, I spend as little time with him as possible."

Devon thanked her for her time and she walked them to the door. Outside, the sound of the infinity pool trickling over its edge accompanied them to the street. Bella walked around her car, checking the tires and the hood. She looked underneath for any leaked fluids.

When they were in the car and driving away, he asked, "You're concerned that someone might be following us?"

"If no one is following us, then the person framing you is a fool, and we both know that's not the case." She hadn't spotted a tail but she had that feeling, that hair-raising prickle that warned something was off.

"We should visit your house manager." Bella merged into traffic.

"If she's home. She took the week off. She may be visiting her sister in Rockford."

"Maybe we'll get lucky and she's relaxing at home."

Mapleton Avenue, Oak Park, 6:20 p.m.

THE USUAL FORTY-FIVE-MINUTE drive to the Oak Park neighborhood took well over an hour in evening rush-hour traffic. On the way, Bella questioned him about Mariah. Did she seem her usual self? Did anything she said set off warning bells? Did she and Richard have an open marriage?

Mariah had seemed the same as always. Lighthearted, friendly, open. Devon had suspected that Richard and Mariah had affairs whenever they chose. But they were always discreet. The only part that had set off warning bells was the one lie he knew for a certainty that she had told him. She had said that Richard was in Wimbledon for the tournament and that was wrong. This year, the games didn't begin until the end of the month. It was possible Richard had told her this lie, assuming she wouldn't bother to verify it, allowing her to believe he would be out of the country to cover his activities.

"Victoria has a contact who can determine whether Richard left the country," Bella said, "assuming he used his own passport. It will take some time, but we can verify that aspect of what his wife said."

"I will be deeply indebted to Victoria for her help." There were few people he trusted as much as he did Victoria Colby-Camp.

"Apparently Richard's financial losses weren't as significant after your partnership dissolved as I assumed."

She spared him a glance as she parked in front of the small home of Devon's house manager, Mrs. Harper. Devon released his seat belt and reached for the door. "I'm confident he considered slipping from a billionaire to a mere millionaire quite tragic."

Bella laughed. He liked the sound of it. "I guess so."

Mrs. Harper's home was a classic early-twentieth-century Craftsman wrapped in tan stucco. The windows and trim were highlighted by green and terra-cotta. The lawn was neat and the flowerpots on the front steps overflowed with blooms.

Bella climbed the steps in front of him. He found himself again admiring her backside. He wondered if it felt as firm as it looked. His fingers itched to test those well-toned muscles.

She knocked on the door. Inside, the sound of a television gave him hope that perhaps his house manager was home. A minute or so passed and Bella knocked again.

Mrs. Harper rarely took a vacation. He generally had to insist. At seventy, she shouldn't push herself so hard. When he'd hired her as head housekeeper, he'd quickly noticed how very good she was at ensuring the entire property was kept in order. If not for her—since Cara had no interest in such things—he would have had his hands full monitoring what the rest of his staff was doing and what was needed. He quickly spotted her organizing ability and offered her the position of house manager over the entire estate. She had refused, insisting she was not qualified. He'd persevered and she'd finally accepted the position and a sizable raise in salary. Last year he'd given her a new SUV as a token of his appreciation. Each year, he gave her something. She was invaluable to him.

Worry edged into his thoughts. If she was home, why didn't she come to the door? Something moved in the front window.

Bella had spotted the movement as well. They both stared at a cat walking along the table that sat in front of the window. At first, Devon thought the white cat had a crimson streak in its fur, but on a closer look, it wasn't a stripe. It was blood. Part of the fur had matted and dried to a darker, rustier red.

Devon grabbed the doorknob and twisted. Locked. He slammed against the wood, using his shoulder like a battering ram. Another hard shove and the door popped open. Inside, the coppery smell of blood and the stench of death were thick in the air. The cat squalled and rocketed across the room.

Bella drew a gun from her bag. Devon stared at the unexpected move. He hadn't realized she had a weapon.

"Call 911."

He withdrew his cell and made the call as he followed her into the kitchen. Gertrude Harper lay in the middle of the room on the beige tile floor, blood pooled around her torso. A large knife protruded from the center of her chest.

"Don't get in the blood," Bella warned. "I'll check the rest of the house."

There was no need to check her pulse. The blood had coagulated. Judging by the condition of her body, the bloating and the bloody foam that had leaked from her mouth and nose, she had likely been dead for at least three days, possibly longer since the air-conditioning was set to a rather low temperature.

He backed away from the body and the pool of blood. He saw no indication of a struggle. The back door was locked, the area around the lock undamaged. He moved back to the front

door and noted the same beyond the splinter-
ing around the lock that had occurred when
he broke in. Whoever had come into her home
and murdered her had been allowed inside. No
breaking and entering. No struggle.

She had known her killer.

The cat peeked from under the table. Mrs.
Harper always talked about her cats. She'd had
several at any given time during most of her
life but she was down to one now. Casper. The
ghost, she had called him.

How long had it been since he'd eaten?

Devon searched the cabinets until he found
the cat food. He emptied a small can into a saucer and placed it on the floor. He wasn't sure
where the water bowl was, so he made a new
one using a cereal bowl.

Watching the cat devour the food, he suddenly felt very tired. Devon sat down on the
floor next to the cat and leaned against the
cabinet. Mrs. Harper was a kind, hardworking
woman who certainly did not deserve such a
violent death. She had grandchildren, a son…a
bloody cat.

Bella came back into the room. She looked at
him for a moment, then crouched down nearby.
"The rest of the house is clean and orderly. I
can't see that anything was disturbed." She put
her arm over her mouth to block the smell. "We

should probably wait outside." She searched his face. "You okay?"

"Of course." He stood. Decided the cat needed another helping, checked the water bowl and then he joined Bella on the front porch.

"I'm assuming Mrs. Harper had the codes to your security system. Keys to your house."

"Yes. She had full access to everything except my personal computer."

"This is how Maynard's belongings got into your house," Bella said. "It's how she knew about the room. You need to call a locksmith and your security company right now."

Feeling wearier than he had in a very long time, Devon made the call. He'd hoped that maybe someone who worked at his home under Mrs. Harper's supervision had caused the breach.

The sound of sirens in the distance sickened him.

Maybe he deserved all of this but Mrs. Harper didn't…the dead mechanic didn't.

Why didn't Richard or whoever the hell wanted something from him just do whatever necessary to take it?

Why all the games?

Why now?

Chapter Eight

Evergreen Avenue, 8:30 p.m.

The Old Town neighborhood had grabbed Bella's heart the first time she strolled along the tree-lined narrow streets with its Victorian buildings and brick alleyways. She'd actually stumbled over the house on Evergreen completely by accident. The historic architecture and classic brick had been exactly what she wanted. Three bedrooms, three baths and an office. Perfect. Plenty of room if her sister and the children ever wanted to visit.

Bella wasn't holding her breath on that one but she could always dream. She and her sister had lost touch after she basically abandoned Bella and then, years later, refused any sort of help financially rather than drifting from one jerk of a husband to the next.

The price of a house in this neighborhood had been difficult to swallow but Bella was frugal in other areas. Her car was not a luxury model. She shopped sale racks at her favorite department stores. Her furniture was an eclectic collection of what she'd already owned and revitalized with unique flea-market finds. It felt like home. She was happy here.

Devon Pierce stood in the center of her small living room and surveyed the decor. His expression didn't show approval or distaste. Her whole house would fit into his west-side parking garage with lots of room to spare. Whatever he thought of her home, she refused to be nervous. This was *her*. She neither needed nor wanted to impress him.

Well, maybe just a little.

"I'll be right back," she said.

He nodded, his attention captured by the framed photographs on her mantel.

She rushed up the stairs to her bedroom. Poking her head into the closet, she dragged her leather overnight bag from the top shelf. She'd had the well-broken-in bag since she graduated high school. Her favorite teacher had bought it for her. The woman had assured Bella that she would go far and she had made her promise to believe in herself.

"So far, so good." Not once since she'd left for college had Bella doubted her ability to rise above where she'd come from. She was more than capable of going as far as she chose, and she refused to believe otherwise. The Colby Agency had given her the opportunity to fulfill herself professionally on many levels. Chicago provided a fresh start with no one to look at her and wonder how she survived, much less thrived.

Until Devon Pierce. He hadn't hidden his surprise in regard to what he'd learned about her past. To her surprise, she had not been intimidated at all by his questions. Impatient, less than thrilled, but not daunted in any way.

All she needed right now were a few things for the next couple of days. She left her overnight bag on the bed while she selected the clothes she needed to pack. Conservative tops, slacks and a couple of lightweight dress jackets. She tossed in her favorite sleepwear. A spare pair of shoes, underthings and her cosmetics bag. She kept a cosmetics bag packed for just this sort of occasion. Often, an assignment would mean travel. Better to be prepared ahead of time than to snatch up items and ultimately forget something like her favorite moisturizer or dental floss.

On second thought, she stuffed the book she'd been reading into the mix and grabbed a box of rounds for her Ruger. The last thing any Colby investigator ever wanted was to have to use a weapon, but sometimes it was necessary. This case was growing more and more volatile. Getting caught unprepared was the other last thing any investigator wanted.

She hefted the leather bag and looked around the room just to be sure she hadn't forgotten anything. "Phone charger." She collected the one from her bedside table and tucked it into her bag. She'd been using the one in the car but it was a hassle to remember to plug her phone in whenever she slid behind the wheel.

Downstairs, Pierce had wandered through the dining room and into the kitchen. She left her bag by the front door and joined him.

"It's not so fancy but it makes me happy."

A rare smile tilted his lips. "It's very homey."

She nodded, not certain whether that was a compliment or an insult. "Thanks."

"There's an abundance of color and a lot of—" he shrugged "—*things*, but it feels inviting and calm somehow."

So maybe it was a compliment. "I feel calm when I'm here."

"You're ready to go?"

"I am."

When they reached the living room, he paused by the fireplace. "May I ask you a question?"

Since he appeared to be taken with the photograph of her and her sister when they were kids—eight and eleven—she imagined the question would be about that night. The one where the only world she'd ever known had vanished down a dark hole.

"Sure."

"Have you ever wished you could go back and change the past? Somehow make it turn out differently?"

The sadness in his eyes tugged at something deep inside her. "There are some things that can't be changed," she confessed. "If given the chance, would I try to save my mother's life in a do-over? No question. Would it have changed the tragedy that was our childhoods? Probably not. My mother, as much as I loved her, was a selfish woman incapable of taking care of herself, much less two daughters. She would have moved on to another no-good man and the cycle would have started over again."

He turned away from the photo. "Is that why you've never married? You're afraid of choosing the wrong man?"

Fire rushed up her cheeks. "I'm not afraid of making the wrong choice, no. I've just never met a man I cared to allow to have that much power over my life. I like making my own decisions and not being forced to cater to someone else's needs."

He looked at her for so long she felt that blush move over her entire body.

"You don't want to be ruled."

She laughed. "Therein lies the problem. I have a boss at work. She respects me. I respect her. I don't need a boss at home. I've yet to see a relationship where the woman doesn't feel *ruled* to some degree. No offense. I just don't feel like I need a full-time man to fulfill me."

"You're a very intelligent woman, Isabella Lytle. But your past rules you whether you realize it or not. Two strong, confident people can have a relationship where mutual respect is a key element, if they choose."

"My past may rule me, Dr. Pierce, but at least I learned from it. Your wife cheated on you. Obviously she didn't respect you nearly as much as you believed."

One eyebrow reared up a little higher than the other. "Perhaps not."

Bella felt like an ass for making such a hurtful assessment. Well, hell.

He'd already put her bag in the back seat and settled into the passenger seat by the time she locked up and descended the front steps. She checked the street and moved around to the driver's side.

As soon as she'd pulled out onto the street, she apologized. "I shouldn't have made such a hateful remark. I was wrong. I have no idea what you and your wife felt about each other. I've never been married. I have no right to judge. The truth is, I rarely do beyond making assessments and conclusions about a case. I was being defensive and that was wrong of me. You have every right to think what you will."

"No apology necessary, Ms. Lytle. What you said is correct. Furthermore, had I respected my wife as I should have, I would have been there for her. She wouldn't have felt the need to seek comfort elsewhere."

Arbor Drive, Lake Bluff, 11:40 p.m.

BELLA ACCEPTED A room a few doors down the hall from his this time. She had no desire to sleep on that rock-hard leather bed again.

Then again, it wasn't designed for sleep.

She shook off the notion and stepped out of the shower. Step by step, she went through her nightly ritual. Blow-dried her hair, checked her cuticles and nails, dabbed on a little moisturizer. It felt good to slip on her preferred sleepwear—lounge pants and a T-shirt. Riffling through her bag in search of her lip moisturizer, she came across the journal. Seated on the bed, she opened it to the last entry she'd read.

Devon hadn't talked about the woman who'd

been murdered, Mrs. Harper. She'd worked for him for a very long time. Bella was certain he must feel some pain at her death, particularly such a violent one. But he'd said nothing. Yet he'd sat on the floor of her bloody kitchen and attended to her cat.

She wasn't sure she would ever understand Devon Pierce.

Or his wife.

Bella turned her attention back to the journal.

Devon made love to me tonight. I tried. I really tried to feel what I should feel. His body is strong and beautiful. He loves me, I know he does. But there are things I will never give him. Children. My heart. He deserves more. For tonight, I allow him to do with my body what he will. He lavishes my skin with his mouth...his hands, and he fills me full. Still, I feel nothing. He is not the lover I want...the one I love.

The idea that he had read that entry made Bella feel ill. This was the woman he'd loved, married and wanted as the mother of his children. The one with whom he had intended to spend the rest of his life. Was this the reason he kept his personal relationships as impersonal as possible now?

Like you, Bella. Pierce had struck a nerve. How would she ever trust anyone after what she'd lived through with her parents, her aunt and uncle and then her sister? How could she dare trust anyone on that level? She had made up her mind long ago that no one would ever possess that kind of control over her life.

Never.

Her stomach grumbled. She groaned. Pierce had offered to prepare dinner but she'd begged off. She'd spent nearly every minute of the past twenty hours with him. She needed some space. She checked the clock. It was nearly midnight. Surely he'd gone to bed by now.

She had to eat. Taking a fortifying breath, she opened the door and stepped into the long hall. No need to take her weapon. He'd set the security system with its new passcode. The locks had been changed. For now, they were secure. His bedroom door was closed. Hadn't it been open when she passed earlier?

Taking her time, she descended the stairs. As much as she loved her little house, she had to admit that this place was breathtaking. She really liked the old-world look and the gorgeous furnishings. Too big, though. Way too big. A dozen children wouldn't be enough to fill all the empty space.

She made it down the stairs without running into him.

So far, so good.

The kitchen was dark. She flipped on a few lights and went to the fridge. Her stomach rumbled some more as she perused the offerings. Since it was so late, she decided on a bagel and cream cheese. Maybe she'd have a glass of wine, too. Balancing the bagel and cheese in one hand, she grabbed the bottle of white wine with the other and pushed the door closed with her foot. She turned to place her goods on the counter and he was there, right in front of her, watching.

The bottle of wine almost slipped out of her grasp. "Jesus, you startled me."

He took the bottle from her. "I'll open it for you."

"Thanks." She managed a smile. Searched her brain for something appropriate to say. "Did you eat already?"

He kept his gaze on the bottle and flinched when she asked the question. She doubted he'd eaten anything unless whiskey counted as a food group. Still, he said, "Yes."

The cork made a little pop as he removed it. He rounded up a glass and poured. She smeared cream cheese on two bagels. When he passed the stemmed glass to her, she shoved a bagel at him. "You lied about eating."

He took the bagel. Stared at it without confirming or denying her assertion. "I keep thinking that I should have called Mrs. Harper and checked on her. I should have asked about her plans for the week." He shook his head. "But if I had, she would have assumed I didn't want her to take the time off." He sighed, the sound forlorn. "No one should die that way. Violently and alone."

Bella resisted the urge to reach out and touch him, to comfort him somehow. "You're not responsible for what her killer did. This is out of your control, Dr. Pierce. Believe it or not, you can't control everything around you."

It was that moment when she realized why he was so distant. Why he had no real personal life. Because he couldn't control it. He would deprive himself of those things before he would risk the pain that came with having less than absolute control.

She bit off a piece of the bagel and chewed, mostly to ensure the wine didn't go straight to her head. When she'd swallowed and washed it down with more of the wine, she said, "You are such a hypocrite, Dr. Pierce."

He'd taken a couple of bites from the bagel but now set it aside. "In what way, Ms. Lytle?"

"You shame me for how I refuse to engage

in a lasting relationship. You analyze me, concluding that I'm afraid of making the wrong choices and ending up like the other women in my family, so I avoid relationships altogether. While you do exactly the same thing. You keep everyone you can't control at arm's length. The only people you allow anywhere near you are your employees and the women you hire to fulfill your sexual needs."

The silence that followed her monologue had her turning up the glass and emptying it. Not nearly enough. She poured herself some more. He took the bottle from her hand before she could set it aside. He drank straight from the mouth of it. Mesmerized by the defined muscles of his throat, she managed to get her own glass to her lips so she could drink.

He set the bottle aside. "You're almost right."

She swallowed a gulp of wine and laughed. "Almost? Where did I go wrong, Doctor? Because I'm not seeing it."

"I don't hire women solely for the purpose of sexual release."

She downed another gulp of wine, hoped it would calm her pounding heart. Or maybe just make her light-headed enough not to care how her foolish body reacted to him.

"I hire them to punish me."

She finished off the wine, set her glass

aside. She must have heard him wrong. "I don't understand."

He reached for her hand. "Come. I'll show you."

She should have resisted. She should have simply said no.

She should have gone back to her room.

But she did none of those things.

She allowed him to lead her along that endless corridor and then down the stairs…to the *room*. His fingers held loosely to hers. Pulling away would have been easy. But she didn't.

The lights were dim except for two spaces, the bed and the horizontal bar where the handcuffs hung from chains.

He'd already shed his jacket and tie. Now he unbuttoned his dark blue shirt. The color, she only now realized, made his eyes more the color of the sea. Her pulse stumbled. "What're you doing?"

She felt dizzy. The wine, she told herself. *So not smart, Bella.*

He cast the shirt aside. Her throat tightened at the sight of his bare, broad shoulders and the exquisite way they crowned a beautifully sculpted chest and then tapered into a lean waist. His ribbed abdomen spoke of rigorous workouts. *Punishment.* The realization came so suddenly she swayed.

He walked over to the dangling cuffs and thrust his hands into them. He pulled downward and the cuffs locked, securing around his wrists with a succinct snap. He looked at her, a gleam of vulnerability in his eyes. "Pick up the whip."

"What?" Only then did she notice the coiled leather waiting near him like a snake ready to stride. She shook her head, aware enough to know the almost-hidden note of desperation in his voice wasn't from sexual need. "No."

"You're afraid." He kept his blue eyes steady on her. "You don't need to be afraid, Bella."

The way he said her name made her shiver, made the nerves all over her body tingle.

"I'm not afraid." Well, maybe she was. She was afraid because heat was roaring through her now. She was on fire. She was tempted, so tempted, but also terrified that she would do this and like it and not be able to stop. Sex play was one thing, but taking advantage of Devon's self-loathing was something completely different.

"Do it. *Now*."

His curt tone made her jump.

Did he really think he could make her do this by snapping at her? "No."

"Then go back upstairs, little girl. This is no place for you." He looked away.

What the…? She was walking toward him before her brain had given her feet the order. She snatched up the whip that lay at his feet, the black leather tool nearly invisible against the obsidian leather floor. She walked around him.

"You're a freak. You know that, right?"

"Yes, I do know that." Those blue eyes were hooded now.

Her throat was so dry she couldn't possibly swallow. Her hands shook and wild sensations rushed through her body. Power, urgency, need, fear… The turmoil whipped through her like a hurricane. "What is it you want me to do?"

"Six lashes."

"You're serious?"

"Do it now."

Hands still shaking, she walked around to his back. Broad, muscled and…scarred. Her breath trapped in her lungs as she instinctively moved closer. She reached out, touched his skin. He tensed, those sculpted muscles going rigid. The scars weren't deep but they were raised ever so slightly and discolored.

"Why?" The word whispered out of her.

"Because I need to feel the pain."

She moved around to face him. She stared at him for a long moment, the whip clenched tight in her hand. "No." She shook her head, her certainty mounting. "You don't *need* to feel the pain. It's just the only way you know to let go of control long enough to feel anything."

"You're a psychiatrist now, are you?"

"No, but I watched my parents torture each other my whole childhood because the pain was the only time when they felt free from the rest of the burden life had dumped on them. What you're doing to yourself is the sexual equivalent of cutting."

"You can't do it," he challenged. "You're afraid. Afraid you'll enjoy it too much. Perhaps as your mother did. Or your sister."

She threw down the whip and slapped him hard on the jaw with the flat palm of her hand.

He shook it off and smiled at her. "Do it again."

Damn him! She'd played right into his ploy. Worse, her body hummed with need and, damn her, she *wanted* to do it again.

"Pick up the whip and show me how bad you can be, Ms. Lytle."

"No." She reached for the hem of her T-shirt. He might have her on fire for him, he might have her ready to explode with need, but he would not rule her. "If we're going to do this, we'll do it my way."

She tossed the shirt onto the floor. His gaze fixed on her breasts. She pushed her lounge pants down her legs and kicked them aside, leaving nothing but the lace panties. Lacy lingerie was her one secret indulgence. Now she waited for his reaction. For him to deny that his body could want something without the pain.

He stared at her, his nostrils flaring, chest rising and falling rapidly.

She moved toward him. When she was close enough, she reached for his fly. He drew away but she had the upper hand since there was only so far he could go. She slid the belt from its loops with a hiss of leather against silk. Then she pulled the button free, carefully lowered the zipper over his hardened body.

She dropped to her knees and removed his shoes, his socks, and then she tugged his trousers down his long legs. His briefs bulged with the desire he would have preferred to deny. He didn't want to enjoy this. She understood now. He wanted to be punished for failing his dead wife. For failing himself.

She walked around behind him, making him tense. She dragged the briefs over his tight backside and down his muscled thighs. Her body sizzled, dampened with need. She knelt down, pulled his underwear free of his ankles. Then she moved in close behind him. She kissed his back, licked the scars. So many scars. He shuddered. Her hands moved up and down his chest, over his ridged abdomen and lower to cradle his heavy cock.

He groaned as she smoothed her palm down the length of him. She kissed and kissed those scarred tracks, all the way down to the cleft of his ass. She made her way around him, kissing and smoothing her hands over his skin, touching him everywhere. And then she latched on to a nipple, sucked hard. He threw his head back and growled.

She sucked and nipped until his cock prodded so hard at her she thought she would come just standing there in front of him. She reached up, touched his face, traced his lips, threaded her fingers into his hair. He was so very handsome.

"Tell me what you want," she murmured.

He moistened his lips. "Nothing."

Fury snapped inside her. She gripped his cock and slid her palm back and forth, smoothing and tugging. "Nothing?"

He closed his eyes and shook his head. "Nothing."

She stepped back, peeled off her panties. His eyes came open and he watched as she walked toward him once more. She reached around his neck and held on while she lifted herself and wrapped her legs around his waist. She pressed downward, forcing his cock against her. The smooth, hard feel of his shaft rubbing against her wet folds took her breath. She was the one to groan this time. She held on tight to him while she rubbed up and down his length, careful not to allow him inside.

The friction, up and down, up and down the shaft of him, stroking harder and harder against her clitoris, her breasts grinding against his solid chest, had her rushing toward orgasm. So close, so close. She no longer cared what he wanted or didn't want. *She* wanted this. To feel him big and hard against her. The first crash of pleasure made her cry out. She rode it out, moving up and down, harder, faster.

And then she came.

He was panting as hard as her, his cock throbbing insistently against her damp folds. She laid her head against his shoulder and shivered with the final remnants of exquisite pleasure.

"You see." She lifted her head, put her lips close to his ear. "I'm not afraid to feel the pleasure without the pain. It's you who's afraid. Call it punishing yourself, call it whatever you like, but it's plain old fear."

His arms tensed as he jerked downward, the cuffs clicked and his hands were suddenly on her back, holding her firmly against him while he strode toward the bed. He placed her in the center of the dim spotlight and moved over her, his face a harsh mask of need.

She reached for his face to pull him into a kiss but he dodged the move. His mouth landed on her breast. He sucked so hard she felt the pull all the way to her core. Then he bit her. She yelped. He bit her again, then moved to the other breast. He sucked and gnawed at her until she undulated beneath him on the verge of coming again.

He pushed her thighs part, pressed the heel of his hand against her and applied just the right pressure. Orgasm crashed down on her.

His fingers dug deep inside her, caressing those clenching muscles. He pushed and tugged, loosening her, finding that spot inside that made her squirm with need. And then he moved onto his knees and lifted her. She couldn't breathe, couldn't think. She was coming again, so hard, so hard. He pushed into her, going so deep she screamed with the delicious ache of it.

He moved slowly. She tried to buck her hips but he held her still. She begged him to go faster but he refused. So slow, so deep, so damned slow. Over and over, he penetrated her, fractured the walls she had built around her feelings, made her want something she could not name.

She cried out with the new waves coming, so very far away. He withdrew to the very tip and then he went in hard and deep, filling her so completely, his body covering hers, pressing her against the leather, skin to skin, his cock so deep he felt a part of her.

They came together and the orgasm went on and on.

When the waves of pleasure had receded, they lay there, sweating and panting for long minutes.

Finally his mouth founds hers and he kissed her.

As certain as she was that her body could take no more, she arched her hips and urged him to take her to that place of pure sensation again.

Chapter Nine

Thursday, June 7, 7:30 a.m.

Devon paced the floor while he waited for the news from Victoria. Bella had been on the phone with her for several minutes.

They had avoided each other since waking. He'd never slept in the room before. He'd lost count of the number of times they'd found release. Total exhaustion had prevented them from moving to his bedroom.

Or perhaps he had felt safer there, less personal.

He shook his head. Not so. Last night had felt intensely personal and incredibly intimate.

More than just sex.

He pushed the thought away and focused on the woman pacing the floor with the cell phone pressed against her delicate ear. Even now, he thought of all the ways he had tasted her—all of her. He knew every part of her, every sweet and salty and lush inch. He had been married to Cara for five years and had not known her so thoroughly, so intimately.

The call finally ended and Bella turned to him. "Richard Sutter has not left the country. Not unless he used an alternate ID."

"Richard is a man of means with extensive contacts. It's possible he left the country as someone else." Devon shook his head. "But it doesn't feel right."

Bella slipped her phone into the pocket of her sleek jacket. She wore a skirt today. It was straight and covered those luscious thighs all the way to her knees. The matching pale lavender jacket and blouse fit well, showing off her curves. The color suited her. She stood in front of the fireplace, the rough stone and rich wood a perfect backdrop for her softness. How could a woman look so soft and fragile and be as strong as he knew her to be? She had commanded his performance last night, drove him and guided him like a maestro leading a world-class orchestra.

"I know what you mean," she agreed, seeming distracted. "Why go to so much trouble to bring you down if he wasn't going to hang around and watch? Has he accomplished what he set out to do? I don't think so. What're your thoughts, Dr. Pierce?"

Dr. Pierce? He crossed the room and stood directly in front of her. "Devon," he said. "You should call me Devon."

She searched his eyes for a moment. "Are you certain that's what you want? Last night we both needed escape, but today is business. If we bring what we did outside that room, then we're starting something different. Is that your intent?"

A vise gripped his chest. Fear. He recognized his old friend. "Point taken, Ms. Lytle."

She opened that sexy mouth but his cell phone interrupted whatever she intended to say. Perhaps it was best.

The display showed a blocked call. "Pierce," he said.

"Help me."

The voice croaked across the line.

"Who is this?"

Bella's face turned questioning, so he put the call on speaker. "Hello?" he said, hoping to prompt the caller to speak again.

"Please help me."

The voice sounded familiar. "Ms. Maynard?"

Bella nodded her agreement with his assessment.

He urged, "Ms. Maynard, where are you?"

"I don't know who she is," said a male voice, taking over the call, "but she's lying on the sidewalk on Shakespeare over here in Logan Square. The old abandoned shoe warehouse. She said she needed help, so I let her use my phone. You better get somebody over here. She might not make it."

The call ended.

"Call an ambulance," Bella said as she rushed away. "I'll get my bag."

ONE HOUR AND thirty minutes later, they stood in the observation area of the surgery unit at the Edge. Devon had called for an ambulance to rush Audrey Maynard here. She'd been badly beaten in the last twenty-four hours. At present, the most pressing issue was the infection at the site of her previous surgery. Dr. Reagan had reopened the original surgical wound and would debride and clean as necessary before closing once more. Close observation and IV antibiotics would be needed until she was out of danger.

Since she was unconscious when she arrived, she had not been able to provide answers to any of the questions Devon or the police had for her. Corwin and Hodge had arrived and were waiting to speak with Devon now.

"Hopefully when she wakes up, she'll be ready to give some real answers."

Devon turned to the woman at his side. "If

she can't or won't give any answers, we're exactly where we were when this whole thing started."

He tried to pinpoint what it was that had set this insanity in motion. There had been no new honors bestowed upon him. No flurry of activity in the news. Nothing unusual at all. It wasn't any sort of anniversary. Not of his wife's death or of when they married or of when his partnership with Sutter began or ended.

The week was like any other except for Audrey Maynard showing up pretending to be his wife and then the murder of his longtime house manager. Part of him wanted to deny the harsh realities. But then that would mean he would have to deny last night. His gaze lingered on Bella. He could not deny what he'd felt last night. For the first time in a very long time, he had felt true pleasure, genuine need.

And he yearned for more.

"We shouldn't keep the detectives waiting any longer."

He stared at her a moment longer. "No matter. We have nothing to tell them."

"They'll have questions. They always do."

The two detectives waited in the small lobby of the surgery unit. Devon invited them to his office, where they could speak in private. As they wound around the corridor to their destination, Bella quietly suggested a seating arrangement to him. Once in his office, he took the seat behind his desk, ushered the two detectives into the chairs in front of his desk, and like the last time, she settled at the small conference table to watch.

"Let's recap a few things," Corwin suggested.

Devon waited for him to begin. He saw no reason to give his permission. The detective was going to say and ask what he would. His comment was simply a way to kick off the conversation and, no doubt, a stab at setting a casual tone.

"The blood in your jacket pocket was a match to the dead mechanic's," Corwin announced.

Devon wasn't surprised. "If the blood in the trunk of the stolen Lexus was his, then of course it was the same as what you found in my pocket. We've established that I inadvertently touched the blood."

"The blond hair found in your house is a match to the hair found in the Lexus driver's seat and in the bed where Audrey Maynard stayed in this ER."

"Detective Corwin," Bella said, "we've already discussed how someone is framing Dr. Pierce. What can you tell us about who that person is? Have you followed up with Maynard's associates? Dr. Pierce's former partner? You must have something more than what you've regurgitated the past few minutes."

Hodge laughed and just as quickly bit his lips together. Corwin did not look amused.

"Your house manager was murdered in her own home, presumably for someone to steal the key to your home since it has not been found. And to get the passcode to your security system."

"Based on my assessment of time of death," Devon argued, "the timing is right. It's the only possible explanation."

"We're considering that avenue as well." Corwin flipped open his small notebook. "Why didn't you tell us about your other partner, Richard Sutter? The one your friend here called the feds about?"

"Mr. Sutter recently battled cancer," Devon told him truthfully. "I saw no reason to cause him unnecessary grief. There, you now know my secret."

"That doesn't explain why you wanted to know if he'd left the country," Corwin countered. "You must suspect his involvement. After all…" He flipped to another page in his notes. "…he filed suit against you three times. If you felt sorry for him, why didn't you toss him a bone and settle? He was your partner when you developed this highly sought-after facility."

Someone had done his homework and spoken to Richard's wife. The entire time she'd been smiling at Devon, she had been hiding the fact that she'd spewed the whole ugly past to the police. Or maybe they'd visited her after he and Bella dropped in. He couldn't be sure of anything anymore.

"Richard Sutter was once a great man with vision, but something happened five years ago and he became a liability. If you had done your homework as well as you believe, you would know Richard received a handsome settlement when we parted ways. The lawsuits that followed were the trivial pursuits of a man suffering from a brain tumor."

Corwin considered that news for a moment. "Is it possible Sutter still suffers from some brain issue that's causing him to go to all these lengths to frame you?"

"Anything is possible, Detective." Devon leaned back in his chair. "If Richard is involved, it's possible his wife is covering for him."

"She did tell us he was out of the country," Bella confirmed. "It might be worthwhile to look into her activities."

Corwin stood. "I'll do that. Meanwhile..." He glanced at his partner, who was still seated.

"...as soon as she's stable, we'll be moving Ms. Maynard to Rush."

"She'll need around-the-clock protection," Bella warned.

"And we'll make sure she gets it," Corwin said. "We wouldn't want to lose her again." He bopped his partner on the shoulder. Hodge shot to his feet and echoed his partner's sentiment.

"Dr. Reagan will advise you as to when the patient can be transported." Devon stood. "Good day, gentlemen."

When the door had closed, Bella moved toward him. "We have some more homework to do as well." She shifted her gaze from the closed door to him. "Assuming you can get away for a few hours."

"When it comes to this investigation, you're the boss."

Heat flared in her dark eyes but she turned away too quickly for him to read whether he'd made her angry...or hot. Just drawing in her scent set him on fire, made him hard. He wanted to lock the door and take her right here, on his desk, against the wall, on the conference table.

He couldn't remember when he had wanted a woman so much.

Not since he first saw Cara. They'd been snowed in at LaGuardia that Christmas. Rather than find a hotel as he usually would have, they'd spent the night in the airport talking. She had been on her way back to Atlanta, where she lived at the time. He'd been to a medical conference in Manhattan and was headed back to Chicago. The next morning they both decided to stay a few more days. A month later they'd got married. He had never been happier in his life. Maybe he would never understand what happened to change how she felt. Or why she'd had so many secrets that didn't include him. Slowly but surely she had killed his ability to feel.

Until now.

Isabella Lytle had ignited something inside him that he wasn't sure could ever be extinguished.

1:00 p.m.

THE REDHEAD WAS the only friend of Audrey Maynard's on the street today. Maybe it was the early hour or maybe the others were in hiding.

"I'm not sure this is such a good idea."

Bella glanced at Pierce. He stared across the street and up the block at the redhead, Jasmine, who was pictured in the photo with Audrey Maynard. She was chain-smoking and chatting it up with two men, both of whom looked like trouble.

"You had your chance," Bella said. "Now it's mine."

From the hospital, they'd stopped by her place and she'd changed clothes. Her tightest jeans and a white tank top that fit like a second skin. She wore a black lacy bra for contrast. The red thongs on her feet wouldn't be worth a flip—no pun intended—if she had to chase down a bad guy or make a run for it, but they gave her that casual look she needed for this approach. Her hair was pulled up into a high ponytail with a colorful scarf tied around it. She lowered the car's sun visor and dabbed on a little lip gloss in the mirror.

"You look like a teenager."

She laughed. "I don't know about that but I don't look like a cop and that's the point." She popped a piece of gum into her mouth.

When she reached for the door handle, he touched her arm. Her skin where his blunt-tipped fingers lay so gently against her tingled. "Be very careful."

"Don't worry." She draped the cross-body purse over her neck. Her Ruger fit perfectly into the small crescent-shaped bag. She'd already tucked her cell into her back pocket. It was just like the good old days undercover. She patted the bag. "I have backup."

He still didn't look convinced but he released her. When she emerged from the car, she felt giddy. It was a little silly that a mere touch would make her feel that way but it did. She'd awakened this morning tender and raw in the most intimate places. Her nipples hardened even now despite being sore from his ambitious attention. Thinking of how deeply he'd got inside her made her shiver. He'd wooed her into positions she'd never heard of, much less tried.

She felt him watching her as she jogged across the street. His clothes covered the scratches and teeth marks she'd left on his skin. She'd refused to use the whip on him but she'd tortured him just the same. She had explored every part of him. Tasted all of him. She licked her lips, wishing she could devour his mouth right here, right now. Last night, he had tasted of heat and that smoky rich flavor of the Scotch he preferred.

The redhead glanced at her as she approached. Bella exaggerated the sway of her hips and chomped her gum. "Hey, y'all." She deepened her Southern drawl.

The redhead looked her up and down. "I don't do chicks."

The two men sniggered.

This close, Bella could see the men's bad teeth and the sores that spoke of drug abuse. Ragged jeans and dirty shirts failed to cover the serious need for showers. Stringy hair poked from under their ball caps. The redhead, on the other hand, looked unusually clean. Skin was clear, muscles well toned. Teeth looked solid and reasonably white for a smoker.

"Not even for two Benjamins?" Bella smiled. "I got a thing for redheads."

The redhead glanced at her two friends. "Go play somewhere else. I've got business."

The two fist-bumped her and moved on.

"That your posse?" Bella asked with a disapproving stare after the two.

"You want to talk or you want to get down to business?" She shifted her weight to the other hip. "I got a room."

"I have my own room." She took the other woman's hand. "I'll take you there."

Red glanced around the block. "You smell like a cop to me."

Bella squeezed her hand. "Trust me. I'm not a cop and you're safe with me."

Red walked to the car with her. Bella opened the back door and they climbed in.

"Hey, I know you." Red looked from Pierce to Bella. "What is this?" Fear glinted in her street-wary eyes.

"We only want to talk, Jasmine," Bella assured her. "Answer our questions and you get the two hundred. That's all we want. Answers."

She exhaled a big breath. "Is this about Layla?"

"If you mean Audrey," Pierce said, "that's correct."

"Is she okay?" She turned to Bella. "She was hurt real bad. I talked to her yesterday but I haven't been able to reach her today."

"Do you know who hurt her?" Bella kept her tone firm.

Red shook her head. "It was some private gig. She was promised big money for pretending to be some guy's wife. She didn't know she was going to end up in the hospital." Jasmine blew out a big breath. "The guy almost killed her."

"What guy?"

She shrugged. "She swears she never saw his face, but I'm not so sure I believe her. Anyway, he beat her up really bad."

"She's back in the hospital," Pierce said. "She almost didn't make it this time. She's very ill."

"Damn it. I told her not to trust the bastard. Anyone who won't show his face can't be trusted. I don't care if he is rich. Rich people don't care about people like us. We're disposable. All he wanted was to use her and now she's sick and hurt. Bastard."

"What about her other friends?" Bella asked. "Would they know who the man was that hired her? Or where she's been staying?"

Jasmine shook her head. "I promised I wouldn't tell. I—"

"He's not going to stop until she's dead," Bella warned. "Whoever he is, he won't risk the possibility that Audrey remembers something about him. Please help us. For her sake. She's your friend. If you want to help her, you need to help us."

Jasmine exhaled a big breath. "After she skipped out of the hospital, she decided to lie low at Talia's place over on Loomis."

"Talia?" Bella prompted.

"Talia Loman. She lives in one of her father's rental houses. He don't have nothing to do with her but he can't bear the thought of her living on the street. I don't think she would have told Talia any more than she told me. I swear Audrey doesn't know who the guy is. She didn't even get a good look at him, but she did say he smelled real good, though. Expensive."

Bella and Pierce exchanged a look.

"Have you heard from Talia in the past couple of days?"

Jasmine shook her head.

Bella dug a Sharpie from her bag. She reached for the other woman's hand, wrote her cell number on her wrist. "If you remember anything, hear anything, let me know." She gave her the two hundred-dollar bills.

"We appreciate your help," Pierce said.

Jasmine shrugged. "'Kay."

Pierce handed her three more one-hundred-dollar bills. "Take the night off and sleep in a good hotel."

And all this time Devon Pierce tried to play it so cold. Like he had no feelings at all.

Liar.

Chapter Ten

Loomis Avenue, 2:20 p.m.

Bella beat on the door a third time.

"If she's here," Devon said, frustrated, "she's not coming to the door."

The small house was silent inside. Outside, the paint was peeling off the siding. Gutters sagged. A couple of windows were cracked, both covered with clear plastic. The grass and weeds were knee-deep. If not for the sagging ceiling-fan blades turning overhead on the small porch, Devon would swear the place was abandoned.

"We should check around back."

Devon descended the porch steps behind her. His thoughts should be focused solely on finding his old friend Richard. Instead, he focused on the way the jeans Bella wore conformed to her amazing ass. He was losing control and she was the reason.

The grass was just as deep in the back. It hadn't seen a lawn mower all season. A broken-down barbecue grill stood on the deck. A couple of abused plastic chairs and a large soup can overflowing with cigarette butts rounded out the outdoor decor.

Bella hurried up the steps and banged on the back door. By the time Devon stood next to her, she had already checked the windows. None had curtains and the old-fashioned roller blinds were only pulled halfway down. The window in the door was divided into nine small panes and revealed a kitchen beyond. No blood on the floor, no body.

"Whatever happened," Devon suggested, "Ms. Loman has apparently gone into hiding."

Bella pulled a glove from her pocket, slipped it on and wiggled the door as she leaned hard against it. "It would appear so," she said casually, as if she weren't doing all within her power to open the door.

When it didn't budge, Devon took her by the shoulders and moved her aside. Even that harmless touch made his pulse react. He turned his back to the door and punched his jacket-clad elbow through one of the windowpanes. The old thin glass shattered.

Before he could do so, she carefully threaded

her arm through the wood frame that once held the pane of glass now spread over the floor inside. Jagged pieces remained around the frame like hideous teeth, making the reach inside precarious.

Bella opened the door and stepped wide over the shattered glass. Devon followed, closing the door behind him.

"Ms. Loman?" she called. "Are you home?"

They moved slowly through the house. No smell of blood. Only the stench of cigarettes and stale beer lingered. The house was sparsely furnished. A well-worn chair and a dingy sofa in the living room. A table with mismatched chairs in the kitchen. A mattress lay on the floor in the first bedroom. No clothes in the closet.

Devon crouched down and looked more closely at what appeared to be a crimson stain in the center of the mattress. "Maynard may have slept here."

"Looks like that's all she left behind."

The final bedroom had the mattress on the floor as well as a couple of boxes overflowing with unfolded clothes. No blood, no sign of the woman who lived here.

"Maybe she helped Maynard to the location where she was found." Bella checked the closet, riffled through the four dresses hanging from the wooden dowel. "She likely recognized that her friend was very sick but needed her away from where she lived before the police were notified."

"That's what friends are for, right?" Devon commented. Frustration tightened his gut. How the hell did these people expect to get help if they didn't report the trouble to the police?

Bella stared at him for a long moment. "Think about how the police are harassing you. How they make you feel in hopes of prompting a reaction. Imagine multiplying that a thousand times. These women are just trying to survive and most of the time they feel like no one is on their side."

"I stand corrected," he confessed. "I'll see that the broken glass in the door is repaired immediately." He withdrew his phone and sent a text to the man who took care of these sorts of issues at his own home. "Done."

Bella walked out of the room. She found the broom and a page from a newspaper and cleaned up the glass. Devon tried to help but she shooed him away.

When he would have attempted another apology, his cell vibrated. Blocked call.

He showed the screen to Bella and then answered, placing the caller on speaker. "Pierce."

"Dr. Pierce, I have information you might be interested in."

Male. Sounded young.

"What sort of information?" Pierce asked. Bella nodded her approval.

"About your wife. You meet me with, say, ten thousand in hand and I'll tell you what I know."

Bella held her phone up for him to see. She had typed: You choose the time and place.

"Four thirty," Devon said. "Lincoln Park Zoo at the seal pool."

"Be sure you bring the money."

"How will I recognize you?"

"I'll recognize you."

The caller severed the connection.

"Good choice." Bella checked the time on her phone. "I'll have my backup investigator watching. He can follow the guy from the zoo. Maybe we'll learn something more that way."

Devon waited on the deck while she locked the door with her gloved hand. "You have backup?" He shouldn't be surprised. The Colby Agency was the best of the best.

"Lacon Traynor. He's on call. If I need him, I let him know. For this, I'll need him."

"I guess we're off to the zoo."

He couldn't wait to see what his enemy had up his sleeve this time.

Lincoln Park Zoo, 4:30 p.m.

THE CROWD WAS THICK.

Bella wished now that Pierce had chosen some other location. There were way too many children here for her comfort. Traynor had sent her a text with a selfie of his location. He was just down a few yards in the front row. She and Pierce had claimed front-row seats as well. Some people chose to stand as the training and the feeding of the seals started.

What she really wished was that he had allowed her to call Detective Corwin. The stakes in this case had grown way too dicey. This man they were meeting was guilty at the very least of extortion and perhaps far worse. At least two people related to this case were dead and another was gravely injured. Bella didn't like this. She didn't like it at all. But Pierce had insisted on doing this his way.

The children cheered and applauded as the seals clapped and barked for treats. A man in jeans, a khaki shirt and blue ball cap wandered over and sat down next to Pierce. Bella watched him from the corner of her eye. He had dark brown hair, and his eyes were concealed with sunglasses. The stubble on his chin could be a fashion statement or an indication of desperation. Judging by how wrinkled his shirt was, *she concluded the latter.* The money their mystery man had requested was in a bag they'd picked up in one of the shops. A T-shirt sporting the Lincoln Park Zoo logo concealed the bales of cash. The bag sat on the ground between them. Both she and Pierce wore zoo caps and sunglasses.

"I wasn't sure you'd really come," the man said without looking at Pierce or at her.

"I'm here and I have what you asked for. You have my undivided attention, so speak."

"Richard is my friend," said the man. He appeared to be in his early thirties. "We've been friends since I interned for him eight years ago. I'm worried about him."

Bella had done a great deal of digging into Richard Sutter. He had a medical degree but he had spent most of his career in high finance and in the development of cutting-edge medical technology. His friend was likely in one of those same fields if he'd interned for the man.

"Why would you be worried about him?" Pierce asked. "And why would it be worth anything to me?"

"Because I…" The younger man turned his face away for a moment. Then he said, "Trust me, you'll find what I have to say worth your time and your money."

"Does his wife know about the two of you?"

Bella cringed behind her sunglasses. Pierce should refrain from trying to piss the guy off until he said what he had to say.

"Probably," the guy confessed. "Richard and Mariah do their own thing. Their marriage is that way."

"Does that include sleeping with my late wife?"

Pierce's lips tightened on the words and Bella wondered if he was still in love with the woman he'd buried all those years ago. Her chest felt tight at the idea, which was ridiculous, but there it was.

"Your wife—Cara—was planning to file for divorce."

Pierce's attention cut to the other man. "How would you know this?"

He shook his head. "I didn't, but Richard did. He told me there were things you didn't know. Cara had a whole different life planned. She was only waiting for the right moment to tell you. She'd planned to do so while the two of you were in Binghamton visiting her family. Cara was not coming back to Chicago with you."

Tension simmered in waves from Pierce. Bella hoped he could keep it together to hear the guy out.

"Richard believes I learned this information and tried to harm my wife, is that it?"

Pierce's words were laced with fury.

"No." The man shook his head. "He doesn't think you had anything to do with her accident, but he's reasonably sure he knows someone who does believe you were responsible."

"Who?"

The single word was uttered so harshly that several people stared at them. Bella put a hand on his arm and gave it a squeeze.

"He tried to warn you that something big was about to happen. He left you a note in your office. Richard knew you would never listen to him, so he left that ominous note in hopes you'd begin your own investigation before all this started."

"Give me the name," Pierce demanded.

The younger man shook his head. "I can't. He wouldn't tell me. He said he had to follow up and sort out a couple of things. That was three days ago. I haven't heard from him since."

Pierce stared forward. "Then why are we here?"

"Richard said if I didn't hear from him within a certain period, I was to assume he was dead and to give you a message."

Bella's heart bumped into a faster rate.

"The only reason I asked for the money was

so you'd know I had important information. I
don't want the money."

His statement was a definite surprise. But
Bella wasn't ready to cut him too much slack
just yet.

Pierce said, "I'm listening."

"Cara was planning a new life with a new
partner. Part of that plan involved an address
you should visit. You'll understand then that
everything you believed about your wife before she died was a lie."

53rd Street, Hyde Park, 6:15 p.m.

THE ADDRESS THE unnamed man had provided
was in the landmark Hyde Park Bank building
on the penthouse floor.

Bella's associate from the agency, Traynor,
had followed the self-proclaimed friend of Sutter's from the zoo. The car he was driving was
a rental.

"Keep in mind," she cautioned Devon as they
rode the elevator to the penthouse floor, "the
elaborate setup with Maynard. This could all
be part of the ongoing smoke and mirrors. Even
when we see what Sutter wants us to see here,
we may not have anything but more lies."

Devon had considered as much. At this point,
the only person he trusted was Bella.

The doors opened into a large space with soaring ceilings and arched windows. The lobby was empty, of course. It was well after business hours. He was surprised the place wasn't locked up tight. Upholstered chairs lined three walls. A table in the center of the room held magazines and brochures. Devon didn't bother riffling through them. He walked straight to the reception desk and stared at the name on the brass plate. *Dana Jordan*. He didn't recognize the name.

"May I help you?"

Devon looked up as the woman walked up behind the desk. She'd appeared from the wide cased opening that led into the dimly lit corridor beyond the lobby.

Bella moved past him and extended her hand. She was still dressed in jeans and a tank but there was no help for that just now. They hadn't wanted to take the time for her to change. "I'm Investigator Lytle and this is Dr. Devon Pierce," she said. "We're here to speak with you about a private matter that may be related to a string of homicides."

Bravo, Bella. Devon could see the older woman's mind working even as worry claimed her face.

"As you can see, we're closed. The office is generally locked by this hour but I'm expecting a client who couldn't come in during regular hours." She glanced at her watch. "I have a few minutes. I'll try to answer any questions you have. My name is Ursula Curtis. I'm the director here." She gestured to the chairs. "Won't you have a seat?"

Bella held up one of the brochures from the table. "This is a private adoption agency."

If she had said this was Santa's workshop Devon would not have been more stunned. There had been no sign on the door other than the suite number. The magazines on the table had been run-of-the-mill women's magazines. But he hadn't bothered with the brochures.

Adoption agency.

"Yes," Ms. Curtis said. "We handle private adoptions for couples who are looking to start a family and for whatever reasons can't or opt not to have biological children."

"Several years ago," Devon said, his chest so tight he could scarcely speak, "my wife may have come to you about adoption."

Ms. Curtis looked at him, evidently picking up on his pain. "I'm afraid our records are private. Did you come with her?"

"His wife is deceased," Bella cut in. "There are two other deaths. We believe they may be connected. Any help you can give us would be most appreciated."

Ms. Curtis drew in a sharp breath as if she'd only just realized they were talking about murder. "Your wife's name, sir?"

"Cara Pierce."

"May I see your ID?"

He showed the woman his driver's license. It annoyed the hell out of him that his hand shook.

"Let's go to my office."

He followed Ms. Curtis and Bella into the corridor. He waffled between anger and shock. Had Cara wanted a child? She'd always told him she didn't. He'd wanted children but he had acquiesced to her wishes.

How could they have lived in the same household and there be so many secrets?

In the director's office, they sat in front of her desk while she searched through file cabinets. Bella put her hand on his arm and squeezed. He couldn't look at her. What kind of man wasn't aware of his wife's most basic desires?

"Cara Pierce." Ms. Curtis withdrew a file and settled behind her desk. She opened the folder and unclipped the photo from the pages stacked neatly in the file.

The photo was of Cara. He remembered that photo. He'd taken it the year before...she died.

"She was looking for a girl baby. Under two years of age." Ms. Curtis studied the photo.

She smiled. "I remember her now. She said her husband was too busy to come but he'd told her exactly what he wanted—a little girl with blond hair and blue eyes just like her. Her friend agreed."

Devon blinked. "Her friend?"

Ms. Curtis smiled. "Oh yes. She brought a friend. A woman, slightly older. Dark brown hair. The two seemed so excited. It was almost as if they were the ones looking to adopt." She blushed. "It's always nice to have supportive friends."

"What about personal information?" Bella asked. "What address did Mrs. Pierce provide?"

Devon's brain wouldn't stop playing the words over and over. *A little girl with blond hair and blue eyes...*

The address Ms. Curtis provided was not the Lake Bluff house. It was some eighty miles away in Ottawa. What the hell had Cara been doing? Had she already started a new life with someone else—someplace else—even before the accident that took her life?

"Do you remember if the friend who was with Cara was this woman?"

Devon pushed aside the tangle of questions in his brain and watched as Bella showed a photo on her cell phone to Ms. Curtis.

"Why, yes. I believe that is the woman who was with her. They appeared to be very dear friends."

Bella showed the photo to Devon before putting it away.

Mariah Sutter.

Devon thanked Ms. Curtis for her help. He couldn't get out of the building fast enough. He felt as if he were suffocating.

Once on the sidewalk, Bella said, "We should confront Mariah with this news."

"Later. Right now I want to see the house where my wife was building her new life without bothering to tell me she was abandoning the old one."

Island Avenue, Ottawa, 8:30 p.m.

IT WAS DARK when they arrived.

Pierce had hardly said a word. Traynor had called. He'd followed the man from the zoo to an upscale loft downtown. He was watching the place until further notice. He'd also heard from Victoria's contact. Jack Hayman had been out of the country for three months. To some degree, that put him in the clear.

Bella parked a few houses away from their destination. The street and the houses weren't what she'd expected. They were small and cute, more like her house, and not at all like the mansion Cara had shared with her husband.

Pierce was already out of the car when she reached for a flashlight in the glove box. She climbed out and said, "We should be careful. The place could belong to someone else now."

He nodded with only a glance in her direction as they walked toward the small white house.

A white picket fence surrounded the house. Pierce opened the gate, the creak sounding far louder in the darkness. There was a streetlight but it was half a block away. White clapboard siding, pale green shutters and a redbrick chimney made up the exterior of the small, two-story cottage. There wasn't really a front porch, more a small stoop. The house was dark inside.

She took Devon's hand and led him around the backyard with nothing but the moonlight to guide them. The narrow backyard backed up to the river. A small seawall and an iron fence separated the two. French doors on the back patio overlooked the water. A small table and two chairs sat in the center of the patio facing a homemade fire pit. It was too dark to tell if it had been used recently without turning on the flashlight.

Devon checked the French doors and they were locked.

Bella turned to the man whose whole world was suddenly on its ear. "We have two choices here. We can go back to Chicago and look into the owner of this property tomorrow when the offices we need to call are open for business." She took a deep breath. "Or we can break the law and go in and see what we find. I don't advise the latter. Any evidence we find would be rendered useless."

They were already in enough trouble for entering Mrs. Harper's home. Considering Pierce was a doctor and the possibility that Harper was gravely injured allowed for exigent circumstances. Not the optimal situation, but justifiable. This time was different. There was absolutely nothing here to show exigent circumstances any more than there had been at the bungalow that belonged to Maynard's friend.

"I'm going in." He reached for a chair.

She grabbed his arm. "Wait a minute. Let's see if there's an unlocked window or a hidden key before we go busting up the place." She pointed to the top of the door. "Check that ledge. Under the welcome mat and under anything else that isn't nailed down."

Bella moved from window to window. All locked or painted shut. "Damn it," she muttered. "Found it."

She turned to see Devon putting a flowerpot

back in place. The idea that a flower with fresh blooms was growing in the pot warned that the place hadn't been deserted for any length of time. If someone was home or arrived before they were out of here, they would have a hell of a lot of explaining to do.

With those concerns ringing in her ears, she joined him at the door as he opened it and then pocketed the key. Bella reached for a wall switch and gave it a flip. A four-arm chandelier that had once been brass but had been painted white glowed to life. Streaks of gold showed behind the white, giving the metal a worn look. It hung over a table with four chairs. The table too had been whitewashed.

The kitchen and dining area overlooked the backyard and the water. The cabinets and counters were white. Small colorful touches of fuchsia, lavender and gray were scattered about. Vintage dishes and well-used cookware were stored in the cabinets along with a few canned and dry goods.

Beyond the dining side of the room was a wide cased opening that led into the living room. The fireplace was small, the brick painted white, though glimmers of the red brick still showed through.

A love seat and a couple of chairs were flanked by tables. None of the pieces were new or matched. The decor was very bohemian. Sheer, gauzy curtains in a crisp white hung on the windows.

There were no photographs anywhere. Devon moved about the room, studying decorative objects. A small wooden bird that had been painted yellow. A white ceramic dish filled with individually wrapped mints. He picked one up.

"These were her favorites. Whenever we had a party, she insisted on having a bowl of these mints."

"Let's have a look upstairs." Bella waited for him to follow.

They climbed the stairs and found two bedrooms and one bath. The first bedroom they encountered had no furniture and was painted a soft pink. White ruffled curtains hung on the windows. The next one had a standard bed with dozens of pillows atop it, with mismatched tables on either side and a long ottoman stretching across the foot of the bed.

A rock sat on one of the bedside tables. The word *happiness* had been engraved into it.

A creak drew her attention around. He had opened the closet door. He pulled on the string and the bare bulb overhead in the small closet turned on.

He touched a silky blouse, then a soft T-shirt. "These are Cara's."

A pair of sneakers lay on the floor of the closet along with an overnight bag. Bella pulled the bag out of the closet and sat down on the ottoman to see what was inside. Underthings, flip-flops and a couple more T-shirts. Bella unzipped the back pocket and found documents. She pulled them from the bag.

Petition for Dissolution of Marriage.

The divorce papers were unsigned.

Devon took the papers from her and flipped through them. The man in the ball cap had been right. Cara Pierce had been in the process of building a whole new life.

Without her husband.

"We should drive back to the city and talk to Mariah again." Bella stood and set the overnight bag aside. "There's nothing else to be learned here."

Pierce handed the pages back to her and she put them away. She didn't bother putting the bag back into the closet.

Bella followed him across the room to the door of the en suite bath. He stood at the sink. Surveyed the array of items scattered about. A jar of moisturizer, an expensive-looking bottle of perfume. A brush. A towel covered in pink and red roses hung over the shower rod that circled the claw-foot tub.

He turned back to the door, his face impassive. "You're right. There's nothing here anymore that matters."

Cara would never be coming back here.

Bella stalled at the bottom of the stairs. She moved aside and waited until Devon had joined her in the living room.

"Look around." She crossed to the coffee table and swiped her fingers across it. "Spotless."

She walked into the kitchen and pulled open the refrigerator. Two bottles of wine. Cheese and grapes. The grapes were fresh. She checked the date on the cheese. "This expiration date is months away." She closed the door and looked at Pierce. "Someone has been here recently."

Someone who had kept every little thing exactly as it was before Cara died.

Chapter Eleven

Clark Street, Chicago, 11:00 p.m.

Mariah answered the door despite the lateness of the hour.

She smiled at Devon. "It's not a good idea to visit a woman when she's so deep into a bottle of wine and at home all alone."

Bella suspected the alone part had been thrown in because of the wine.

"It is late," he agreed, "but it would mean a great deal to me if you could give us a few more minutes of your time."

The older woman's eyebrows rose ever so slightly. "Is that humility I hear in the great Dr. Pierce's voice?"

Oh yes, she was definitely feeling the wine. "It's very important," Bella put in, hoping to prevent the frustration that claimed Devon's face from making a louder appearance. "We've discovered new details you may be able to shed some light upon."

Sadness overtook Mariah's cocky expression. "Oh."

She drew the door open wider in invitation. Then, without another word, she turned and walked deeper into the house, teetering on her high heels just the tiniest bit from the level of alcohol in her blood.

Pierce closed the door and they followed the path the lady of the house had taken. She'd already curled up on the sofa, her emerald-colored silk robe gathered around her like a queen's cloak.

"Feel free to make yourselves a drink," she offered. To Devon, she added, "You know where everything is."

He glanced at Bella and she shook her head. "Thank you," he said, "but we have a long drive ahead of us."

Mariah's eyebrows rose once more. "Really. Your associate is staying with you, then."

"My agency provides protection as well as investigative services," Bella felt compelled to explain. Even as she did so, she felt heat spread across her cheeks.

"Really." Mariah made a wry expression. "Interesting." She sipped her wine before settling her attention on Devon. "What is it you want to talk about? Cara, I presume."

He nodded. "Were you aware she was looking into adopting a child?"

A quiet knowing filled the room. All three knew the truth. There was only the matter of why. The news obviously weighed heavy on Devon Pierce. Bella felt the pain emanating from him.

No matter that his wife had been dead for more than six years and that he had reconciled himself to the reality that she'd had an affair. Finding all the rest—the visit to the adoption agency, the house on the lake and the divorce papers—was like tearing open an old wound and then rubbing broken glass into it. It cut. Deeply.

"Yes." Mariah looked away a moment. "She wanted a child but she didn't want to carry a child." She sighed. "Cara could be very selfish, as I'm sure you recall."

Devon said nothing. He waited, silent and brooding, for her to continue.

"She was an amazing woman." Mariah smiled. "You loved her." She tilted her head and studied Pierce. "I know you did. She knew this as well. But she wanted more than what you had to offer. Sometimes…" Her gaze turned distant as if she were remembering something only she knew. "Sometimes I think she wanted too much." She shrugged. "It's difficult to capture a free spirit and even harder to hold on to it for any length of time."

"Did you know about the cottage in Ottawa?"

Her philosophical expression shifted into a frown at his question. But in that brief moment before the frown took over, Bella spotted the surprise. Whatever Mariah Sutter was about to say was a lie.

"What cottage?"

She sipped her wine, careful that her gaze stayed clear of Devon's and of Bella's. She knew about the cottage. Her surprise was in hearing that he had discovered it.

"A small cottage on the water in Ottawa. Some of her things are there." He sat forward, his forearms braced against his spread thighs, hands dangling. "The place was spotless. As if she'd just walked out the door moments before we arrived."

Mariah shook her head, downed the remainder of the wine in her glass. "There must be some mistake. Cara never spoke of a secret hideaway."

"Someone knew," Devon argued. "Someone *knows*. The food in the fridge was fresh."

"You're serious." Mariah's face cleared of

readable tells. "How can you be sure the place is—was—Cara's?"

"The divorce papers she had drawn up were there. Her perfume and other things were there."

"Oh my God." Mariah shook her head. "It's Richard. He must have bought the place for her. That son of a bitch."

Bella waited for Devon to respond. His body had tensed. His intent gaze focused on Mariah. "What do you mean?"

Mariah sighed. "Good God, surely you recognized that Richard was obsessed with her. He adored her. He probably bought the place for her so she could have her own space away from you. Bastard." She shook her head. "He wanted her all to himself. I guess that's where they held their secret rendezvous."

"You're saying," Bella ventured, "that you believe your husband was having an affair with Cara."

"Of course he was."

"If that's true," Bella countered, "how did the two of you remain so close? Did you not know when Cara was alive?"

"I knew." She set her empty glass aside. "By the time I realized, we were inseparable." She glanced at Devon. "You remember. We did everything together. Richard and I never had children. The two of you appeared to be following that same path." She turned to Bella then. "Our husbands were both completely absorbed in their work. We were each other's salvation."

When Mariah didn't say more, Bella prompted, "How did you remain friends after you discovered the affair?"

"How could you bear to look at her?" Devon demanded.

Mariah shrugged. "We do what we have to do. You know the old saying—keep your friends close but your enemies closer."

"You said Audrey Maynard," Bella said, moving on, "the woman in the photo we showed you earlier, was one of Richard's assistants. How can you be sure?"

She shook her head, gave a half-hearted shrug. "I dropped by the office one day and she was there. He told me she worked for him." She laughed a self-deprecating sound. "Apparently the joke was on me. After what you just told me about this cottage and considering how much this Maynard woman looks like Cara, perhaps he's using her as a replacement. A surrogate of sorts."

Not a completely implausible scenario.

"Do you know a Kevin Unger?" Devon asked.

Traynor, Bella's backup, had called to say

the man who had met them at the zoo had dropped off the rental and picked up an older-model BMW. The Beamer was registered to a Kevin Unger. Traynor had sent her a photo taken from Unger's Facebook page. Definitely the guy from the zoo.

Mariah thought about the name for a moment, then nodded. "Yes, of course. He was an intern for Richard years ago. Before Cara's death, I think. I'm not sure what became of him."

"Their relationship was purely professional?" Devon inquired.

"That was my impression but I can't say for sure," Mariah confessed. "Richard has always been very adept at keeping his personal and professional lives separate, but if you're asking me if the two could have had an affair, it's possible, yes. Richard has had many lovers, female and male."

Devon stood. Bella did as well.

"Thank you again," he said, "for your time."

Mariah dropped her feet to the floor and stood. "You really never recognized what sort of man Richard is." She laughed. "He's even worse since the cancer scare. He's rarely home. Ignores his work. I don't understand what's happening to him."

"If he comes home or calls," Devon reminded her, "I need to see him."

"I'll give him the message."

When they were in the car and driving away, Devon said, "I find it difficult to believe that I misread the man so completely."

Bella held his gaze a moment before pulling onto the street. "Maybe you didn't."

Arbor Drive, Lake Bluff
Friday, June 8, 2:00 a.m.

DEVON STARED AT the drink he'd poured.

He'd been staring at it for half an hour or more. Closing his eyes, he thought of the way the silk blouse hanging in that damned closet had smelled—like her. The perfume she'd always worn had been on the counter in the bathroom.

His wife had been starting a new life.

One that did not include him. She wanted to adopt a child. A little girl. She'd already painted the spare bedroom pink.

Devon swore and snatched up the drink. He downed the Scotch in one swallow. When he found Richard, he would have the whole truth. All these years, he had regretted on a personal level that he'd had to cut Richard out of the project. But like Jack Hayman, the fool had wanted to take shortcuts. He'd wanted to make a higher return for his investment.

The Edge was about saving lives. Of course, some amount of profit was required, but that profit must be reinvested into the facility. Men like Richard Sutter and Jack Hayman didn't have the heart for the project. Devon should have seen his error well before the situation grew ugly.

He licked his lips, hating the weakness that had permitted him to surround himself with people who would betray him.

Pushing to his feet, he reminded himself that he could not change the past. What was done was done. But he wanted—no, he needed— Richard Sutter to look him in the eye and tell him the truth.

Why the hell had he suddenly decided to torture Devon with Cara's death? What had happened in recent months? He'd dropped the last of the lawsuits three years ago. Why attempt to dig at Devon in this new way?

He thought of Mariah's words about Richard not being the same since the cancer. But he had fully recovered. Why suddenly decide to dig up all the ugliness again? Why commit murder?

Whatever he thought of Richard, he would never have believed him capable of murder. If Richard's protégé could be believed, someone else was attempting some sort of revenge against Devon. Hayman? None of it fit. If Hayman or anyone else wanted revenge against Devon for some presumed wrong, why not take it directly against him? Why go to these elaborate extremes?

He went to the bar and poured himself another Scotch.

"You're not going to find the answer in that bottle."

"Perhaps not, but at least I'll no longer care."

Whoever had set this plan in motion had killed at least one innocent person as well as the mechanic who had possibly been involved. Mrs. Harper's daughter had arrived in Chicago. Devon had assured her that he would take care of all the funeral expenses as well as the necessary cleanup at her home as soon as the police released it. Detective Corwin had allowed him to have a veterinarian pick up Casper and attend to him. The cat was unharmed. A good bath was all he'd needed. Mrs. Harper's daughter would take him home with her.

"Apparently you care more than you'd like people to know," Bella noted. "Detective Corwin told me you had called the hospital and insisted on paying for Audrey Maynard's care."

He shrugged. "I'm the reason she was injured. It was the least I could do."

"You shouldn't look at all these new discoveries and see your failure. Sometimes it doesn't matter what we do—we simply can't please the people we love the most."

He lifted the glass but hesitated before taking the drink. "I'm weary of being the topic of conversation, Ms. Lytle." He shifted to stare directly at her. "Let's talk about you. Do nightmares from your childhood wake you up at night?"

"Ms. Lytle." She laughed and gave her head a little shake. "After last night," she went on, her tone frank, her expression open, "I think we're well enough acquainted to dispense with the formalities. Besides, my friends call me Bella. We had this conversation already."

He did take a swallow of the smooth, smoky flavored whiskey then. "Am I your friend, Bella? Fair warning—I seem to have trouble keeping friends. They generally run screaming or furious from our encounters."

Tendrils of her hair had fallen loose from the ponytail she'd arranged it in this morning. He liked her hair down. Liked it up, too. His mouth felt dry, so he downed another swallow of Scotch.

"I'd like to think that we're friends." She picked up a glass and poured a finger of Scotch. "You're still the client and I'm still the hired investigator, but I don't see any reason why we can't be friends. Do you?" She brought the glass to her lips and indulged in a small sip.

"Friends play together, don't they, Bella?"

She licked the alcohol from her bottom lip. "They do."

He placed his glass on the counter and reached for hers. "I would very much like to play with you now."

She downed the trace of Scotch left in her glass and then handed it to him. "Only if I get to make the rules."

"All right."

She led the way. He followed, already growing hard simply watching her move. She appeared so reserved but he already knew that was just for show. He had experienced the wicked wildcat beneath all those prim layers.

When she moved into the entry hall and started up the stairs, he hesitated. "Where are you going?"

She glanced back. "My choice, remember?"

He had agreed to permit her to make the rules.

Upstairs, she walked into his room and turned on the light. When he'd joined her, she closed the door and locked it, then leaned against it.

He glanced around the room. Tension rippled through him. He had not made love in this room in nearly seven years. Not long after Cara was gone, he'd had her things removed... the bed and the linens replaced. Not because he could bring himself to hate her but because he could not bear to see them, to touch them.

Now he settled his attention on the woman watching him all too closely. "What would you like to play?"

"Bella Says," she announced. "Sort of like Simon Says, only different."

Anticipation strummed through him, chasing away the doubts for the moment. "As you wish. What would you have me do?"

"Take off your clothes."

"Not particularly original," he teased. He'd left his jacket downstairs. He removed the cuff links, crossed the room and dropped them onto the table next to the bed. Then he reached for the buttons of his shirt, releasing them one by one. She watched, her respiration picking up. The rise and fall of her full breasts was mesmerizing. He shouldered out of the shirt, allowed it to slip down his arms and fall to the floor.

Her gaze roved over his torso. He held very still, his arms hanging at his sides, and allowed her to look until she had her fill.

"Everything," she clarified.

The shoes came off next. He peeled off his socks, first one and then the other. Reaching to his waist, he pulled the leather belt from his trousers, let it join the shirt on the floor.

She watched his every move, her body growing restless. Watching her watch him made him want to rush to where she stood and take her right there against the door. Instead, he unfastened his fly and removed his trousers. He tugged his briefs down his legs and off. His cock stood fully aroused now. His entire body strummed with need.

For a minute, she studied him, her gaze moving over his body. He waited patiently. Whatever she wanted that was his to give, he would give. So many years had passed since he had yearned to please someone the way he wanted to please her.

Finally, when he could no longer bear the anticipation, he demanded, "What now?" His voice was taut and rough. He ached to touch her.

She pushed away from the door and moved slowly toward him. When she stood directly in front of him, she reached up and removed the scarf from her hair. "On your knees."

He didn't hesitate. He lowered to his knees, his heart rocking against his sternum.

She tied the scarf around him like a blindfold. The lack of visual stimuli was like an aphrodisiac—it only made him harder.

"Stand up."

He did as she asked, hoping she would take him by the hand and lead him to the bed. He wanted to be inside her now. He wanted to taste all of her this second. He quieted the excitement building inside him and listened. She was either standing still or she'd removed the thongs so that he wouldn't hear her steps. He listened intently. The slide of fabric told him she was removing her clothes. The soft whoosh as they hit the floor, piece by piece, sent tremors rocking through his body.

She came closer. He could smell her soft skin. His breath came in short choppy bursts. His cock throbbed for her.

Her fingers slid over his back. She traced a path over his skin, lingering in places that made him groan with need. He wanted to touch her so badly. He fisted his fingers. As if she'd recognized what he wanted, she moved away. Where was she? He couldn't hear her...could no longer smell her sweet skin.

When she returned, she pulled his wrists together behind his back and tied them with a band of silk, perhaps one of his neckties. She reached up to check the blindfold and her body brushed his, the friction of her skin against his lighting a fire over every inch she touched.

He wanted to reach for her but his hands were tied. "That was rather unsportsmanlike of you." He wished he could see her.

"Tell me what gives you pleasure, Devon."

Her voice made him tremble. He gritted his teeth against the weakness. "The whip. Pain."

"Liar."

She clasped his thighs. Only then did he realize she was kneeling in front of him.

"Tell me what you want," she murmured.

He refused. What happened the other night was an anomaly. He never allowed himself the pleasure without the pain. He didn't deserve it. However much he wanted her, he didn't deserve her.

Her hot, lush lips closed over the head of his straining cock. He shuddered.

She squeezed his thighs with her soft hands while her hungry mouth drew on him, took him in deeper. Her fingers found their way to his ass and squeezed until he growled. He jerked at the restraint. Needed to touch her.

And then she stood and stepped away from him. The cool air on his heavy cock had him gasping. He felt her moving around him but she didn't touch him. Had she taken him to this edge only to leave him there, wanting, needing more?

He felt a tug on his arm and he stumbled forward. He followed the tugs. She slipped around him and released his hands. His arms fell to his sides, his fingers aching to touch her.

"On your knees," she ordered. She was in front of him again.

He dropped to his knees. Licked his lips in anticipation of a taste of her.

She grabbed two handfuls of his hair and pulled him forward. His face landed between her thighs. He feasted on her soft folds. Relished the taste of her. Wanted her to feel the same frenzy he had felt. He licked and suckled until she cried out. He used his tongue to penetrate her, to delve as deeply as possible. Slowly, he began to kiss his way up her body, but she scrambled away. He tried to follow, bumping his knee and losing his balance.

He caught up with her on the bed. Her legs were open in invitation and he moved between them and burrowed deeply into her. She was so damned hot and wet and nicely snug. She wrapped her legs around his and lifted to meet his thrusts. He wanted to see her, but the blindfold was still in place.

He leaned down, needed to kiss her. She tore the blindfold away. He blinked at the light, forced his eyes to focus so he could watch her face as she lost herself to orgasm. He closed his mouth over her breast, suckled and nibbled until she was writhing again. He moved to the next one all the while thrusting slowly in and out of her.

He dropped his head to her chest. God, he was so close…so damn close.

"Turn over," he murmured. He desperately needed to be deeper inside her. He needed her to take all of him.

"Beg," she said, her skin flush with her own need. Her breasts plump and jutting forward as if pleading for more of his attention.

"Please," he urged, "I need to be deeper inside you."

She flattened a palm against the center of his chest, held his gaze a moment as she felt his heart pounding, and then she rolled over.

"Arch your bottom for me."

She didn't move. Just lay there with that firm, rounded ass tempting him beyond all reason.

"Please, arch your bottom for me, baby," he pleaded.

With her shoulders against the bed, she lifted her bottom up to him. He nudged her urgently. He guided himself inside and he slid deep, deep into her. He groaned with the intensity of it. It felt so damned good.

Slowly, slowly, he moved inside her. Every ounce of willpower he possessed was needed to restrain his movements. In, an inch, then two, three. Deeper, deeper, until he had given her all he had to give. He felt the muscles inside her start to clench around him. He moved faster until she screamed with orgasm again. He fought to restrain his release. Just a little longer.

She suddenly scrambled away from him, leaving his pulsing cock damp and aching for release. He made a small, strangled sound at the loss of her tight heat. She got onto her knees, facing him. "I want you to look at me. To *see* me."

He kissed her face. "I see you." Kissed her eyes, her nose, her neck and shoulder. He ached so for relief that his entire body shuddered. When he could take it no longer, he grabbed her. He dropped into a sitting position and pulled her over his lap. She went down fully onto him, taking him in even deeper than before. She held him tight against her and rocked and rocked until they both screamed with release.

And then he did something he had not done in more than six years. He pulled her into his arms and held her until they lost themselves to the exhaustion.

Chapter Twelve

6:15 a.m.

Bella watched Devon sleep. The soft morning light trickled in between the slats of the shutters. Stubble darkened his square jaw. The mask of tension he wore more often than not was relaxed. Dark lashes rested against high cheekbones. Her gaze slid down, over his slightly off-center nose, to lips that had teased and tasted every part of her.

Down farther still, she noted the muscles of his neck and then the hard ridges of his chest. Her fingers itched to touch him. To slide beneath the white sheet that lay across his waist. The ferocity and desperation of his lovemaking was every bit as intense as the man himself.

A man who had been deeply wounded on multiple fronts. Betrayed by the woman he'd loved and by a friend and business partner.

Bella thought of the last journal entry she'd read and it made her ache for this man.

The need is insane. I feel addicted and I cannot resist. A moment away from my lover is like a moment without air. It leaves me gasping and desperate. We've made our decision. Our old lives are no longer relevant. Now we move on to the beautiful future that is ours alone. I cannot wait to begin this new journey. Nothing... no one else matters. Only us, and our wonderful plans. Tomorrow I will tell my husband that I'm leaving. I refuse to waste another day on this empty marriage.

The words had been brutal.

Devon Pierce was a victim. Perhaps not in the criminal sense, but in a deeply personal one.

She mulled over the many journal entries she had read. It was clear Cara wanted to conceal her lover's identity. The failure to label the person as male or female seemed unreasonably cautious. It wasn't as if Richard Sutter was the only man with whom she was in contact in the city of Chicago. And if her lover was Richard, why would he send his protégé to warn Devon? Why write that message that seemed to foreshadow coming events? More important, why behave so secretively? If Richard knew the person seeking revenge against Devon, why not tell him or, if he wanted Devon to suffer for his own reasons, why get involved at all?

Unless he was covering for someone who mattered to him on some level.

Bella's heart started to pound. *Mariah Sutter.*

Devon's eyes opened and he immediately turned to her as if he'd felt her watching him. "Good morning."

"Good morning to you." She smiled. "I'm starving."

He rolled over, pressed her against the mattress. "So am I." His mouth came down on hers and he kissed her long and deep, filling her with the taste of him and instantly chasing away her hunger for anything else.

When he came up for air, she whispered, "We should talk about—"

"In a minute." He burrowed between her welcoming thighs and thrust into her.

She gasped and, despite all the places so tender from last night's hours of lovemaking, her body instantly started to move in time with his. The feel of his muscled chest rubbing against hers had her breasts hard and aching. She lifted her hips to allow his thrusts to deepen.

The rattle of her cell phone against the table next to the bed was a distant nuisance. She couldn't have stopped if her life had depended upon it. Her nails dug into his back as the pace escalated. Suddenly she was coming. She screamed with the intensity of it. He growled as he followed her over that edge.

As soon as she could think again, she dragged her cell from the table and checked the screen. Unger had left his downtown loft and Traynor was following him.

"News?"

She rolled onto her side and propped her head on his chest. "Unger is on the move. Traynor is keeping tabs on him."

His relaxed and sated expression vanished and the tension was back.

"There's something else," she said. When his gaze connected with hers, she went on, "I don't think it's Richard. In fact, I don't think he's the one who was having the affair with Cara."

"We've basically ruled out Hayman." He absently stroked her hair, his face a study in concentration. "I can't see Unger being the one."

Bella waited until he looked at her once more. "I think it's Mariah."

His raised eyebrows spoke loudly of his surprise. "That's a hell of a leap from where we've been going with this."

"She was so precise with her thoughts on how her husband felt about Cara. Yet I heard no anger in her voice. When you mentioned the cottage, there was a glimmer of surprise but not a what-are-you-talking-about expression. She knew about the cottage. She went with Cara to the adoption agency. What man would keep the cottage so perfectly spotless and eat cheese and grapes and drink wine? I'll bet Richard is a Scotch man, like you."

"You're right. Scotch is his preferred drink. I picked up my taste for Scotch from him."

"We need to be watching Mariah."

Her cell started that incessant vibrating again. This time it was a call from Traynor. Bella answered with, "What's going on?"

"Our friend Unger lent his car to a neighbor," Traynor explained. "I followed the guy to his office, but now I'm headed back to Unger's place. I'm guessing he won't be there."

Damn it. Without eyes on Unger, they might never locate Sutter.

Clark Street, Noon

"As a detective, I suppose you spent some time on stakeouts."

Bella shifted her attention from the driveway half a block up. They hadn't spent a lot of time talking since they parked on the street that ran in front of Mariah Sutter's house. The driveway exit a few yards away was her only way in and out of the property. If she went anywhere, they would know it.

When they first arrived, Devon had called her home landline to ensure she was in the house. He'd used the excuse that he'd forgotten to ask if she'd heard from Richard. She assured him she had not. Then she'd gone on to remind him of how Richard spent hours on the golf course and in pubs when traveling in Europe. He rarely called home or checked his phone.

Like Bella, Devon wasn't buying it.

"I did my time on stakeouts." She turned back to the street. "Sometimes it was boring as hell and others it was oddly interesting."

"You're a very strong woman, Isabella Lytle." He made this statement without looking at her. "Few could have overcome a childhood such as yours and gone on to accomplish so much."

"I was lucky. I had a couple of really encouraging teachers."

"I suspect luck had very little to do with the outcome."

She turned to him. "Thank you. It wasn't always easy but I never allowed myself to believe any other outcome."

He held her gaze for a long moment. "How did you ever learn to trust again after the way your parents let you down? And your sister, she basically left you to fend for yourself."

Bella hugged herself, feeling suddenly cold. They'd turned off the engine and put the windows down. The air was still reasonably cool after the overnight low in the midfifties. Even in the hottest days of summer, the past could give her an abrupt chill that way.

"I was angry with her at first. I felt like she'd abandoned me." She shrugged. "That she should have stayed and protected me. Eventually I got over it. She killed our father to protect me. She's had to live with that and I'm certain it hasn't been easy. I can't resent her for feeling like she'd done her part. In truth, she had. He would have killed us both."

"I'm surprised you're not more angry with the world at large." He assessed her a long moment. "People seem to need to blame someone for their misfortunes."

"I had no say in what I was born into. It wasn't the world's fault. It was my parents'. They made their choices and we had to live with them. What I chose to do with my life from that point forward was no one's decision but my own. Any blame from that moment lies with me."

"I like the way you think." He smiled.

"I like the way you smile," she said before she lost her nerve. "You don't smile nearly enough." She put her hand on his and savored the texture of his skin.

"It's been a long while since I had something to smile about." He reached out and traced a gentle path on her cheek. "Despite the circumstances, I'm glad we met."

She captured his hand in hers and gave it a squeeze. "Me, too."

The moment passed and they stared forward once more. Eventually their fingers slipped apart.

"Do you feel Mariah would be capable of murder?" Bella asked. For now, they needed to remain focused on the investigation. All these confusing personal feelings would have to wait. "Two people are dead. The mechanic was shot with a small-caliber handgun and Mrs. Harper was stabbed. Could she commit such up-close violence?"

Devon shook his head. "I wouldn't have thought so. But then I was just as certain Richard would never go that far. What about Maynard? She says she was hired by a man. Would Mariah have trusted anyone to carry out those steps or maybe there's another body waiting to be found?"

Bella nodded once. "Maynard spewed a great deal of detail, much of which was untrue."

He rubbed a hand over his clean-shaven jaw.

"We can't say with complete certainty that Hayman, though out of the country, isn't the mastermind behind all this."

"As true as that is, we've found no connection to him so far. Everything seems to connect back to the Sutters."

A car parked on the street behind them. Bella watched in the rearview mirror as Lacon Traynor climbed out.

"It's Traynor." She glanced at Devon. "He must have an update he felt he needed to share in person."

Bella hit the unlock button and Traynor slid into the back seat. He was Bella's age with beach-boy blond hair and sandy-brown eyes. He hailed from Texas and she had decided you could take the man out of Texas but you couldn't take Texas out of the man. His jeans and button-up shirt were complemented with a lightweight sport jacket but there was no mistaking those boots for what they were—well-worn cowboy footwear.

"Still no sign of Unger?" She doubted finding him would be easy but she could hope.

"He's in the wind." Traynor glanced at Devon. "I had a look around inside his apartment and it appears as though he packed a hasty bag. He'd gone through drawers and left a bit of a mess. We may not be seeing the guy again."

"Devon Pierce," she said, "this is Lacon Traynor, my backup detail from the agency."

Traynor reached across the seat and shook Devon's hand. "I got a call from Ian."

Ian Michaels was at the top of the food chain at the Colby Agency. He had been with Victoria for many years. "Was he able to locate the car and driver who picked up Maynard?"

Traynor gave her a nod in the rearview mirror. "Belongs to a car service. The driver is MIA. He hasn't come to work in two days. I checked his home address. Neighbors stated they hadn't seen him in a couple of days."

Bella imagined his body would show up next but she kept the conclusion to herself. Devon was dealing with enough right now.

As if fate wanted to show her things could always be worse, Devon reached into his jacket pocket and withdrew his cell. "It's the Edge." He answered and listened for a couple of beats.

Tension coiled in Bella's stomach. She'd almost suggested that he beef up security at the facility. So far, no attempts to damage or destroy property had been made against the facility, but that could be coming. At this very moment, in fact.

"I'll be right there."

When he put the phone away, he turned to Bella. "It's Unger. He's waiting for me in my office. Patricia is concerned there's something wrong with him but he assures her he's fine, that he just needs to see me."

"I can take over here," Traynor suggested.

Bella didn't want to separate from Devon, but she needed to keep an eye on Mariah. Her instincts were screaming way too loudly for her to risk turning her back on the woman.

"I'll stay here," she countered. "You take Dr. Pierce to the Edge. I'll keep both of you posted on what's happening here."

"No." Devon shook his head. "You should be with me."

Bella felt her cheeks redden. "I'm on the right track with Mariah," she argued. "This is too important to risk letting her out of my sight. If she sees me, I can easily make up an excuse that I have more questions. If she sees Traynor, she'll be spooked."

"She has a good point," Traynor tossed in. "Lytle can take care of herself, Doc. Trust me. I've gone to hand-to-hand classes with her. She kicked my ass."

"Fine." Devon looked at her one last time before climbing out of the car.

Bella watched in the rearview mirror as they climbed into Traynor's car. Then she shifted her attention back to the home of the woman she suspected was a coldhearted murderer.

The Edge, 1:45 p.m.

TRAYNOR PARKED IN the spot reserved for the administrator. "Those friends of yours?"

Detectives Corwin and Hodge emerged from their nondescript sedan, swaggered to the sidewalk and waited, their attention fixed on Traynor's sedan.

"The two detectives who want to pin all this on me rather than find the true perpetrator." Devon reached for the door. Ignoring the two would be futile. The sooner he allowed them to throw a few more accusations at him, the sooner he could go inside and learn what Unger had decided to share with him this time.

"Fun, fun," Traynor muttered.

"Your secretary told us you wouldn't be in today," Corwin said, his tone openly accusing as Devon approached him. "We were just about to leave."

"I hadn't planned to but when you work with emergencies you never know when your schedule will change." Devon struggled to retain his patience. Enough was enough and he'd passed *enough* a considerable time ago. "What can I do for you, gentlemen? I have matters to which I need to attend."

"Well, we have a few matters, too," Hodge

said. He glanced at his partner. "You want me to tell him or you want to tell him?"

Devon resisted the urge to punch one or both.

Corwin narrowed his gaze at Traynor. "Who's your friend? What happened to the pretty one?"

"Lacon Traynor." He thrust his hand at Corwin. "The Colby Agency. My associate had an appointment. I'm standing in for her."

Corwin shook his hand. "Oh, another one of those."

Traynor gave Hodge's hand a shake as well.

Devon was ready to shake the whole lot of them.

"You had something to discuss with me?" he snapped.

Hodge frowned. "I guess we should get on with it. The doc sounds a little testy."

"Your housekeeper," Corwin began.

"House manager," Devon corrected.

"Whatever." Corwin shrugged. "We found a copy of what looks like some kind of diary or journal." He hitched his head toward the car and said to his partner, "Get the evidence."

A chill settled deep in Devon's bones. He clenched his teeth to keep the frustration from boiling out. He shouldn't be surprised that a copy of Cara's journal had shown up. The person or persons behind this insanity were pulling out all the stops.

Hodge returned with a large, clear plastic bag with a stack of white paper inside. He handed it to Devon. His late wife's gentle strokes filled the page on top. He tossed it back to the man. "This is a copy of my wife's journal. I have no idea why Mrs. Harper would have made a copy."

Corwin shrugged. "Blackmail, maybe?"

"I was not being blackmailed by Mrs. Harper or anyone else." Anger tinged his words this time. If only this were as simple as blackmail.

"Well." Corwin passed the bag back to Hodge. "Whether you are being blackmailed or not, that journal shines a whole new light on the relationship between you and your wife."

"Thing's chock-full of motive," Hodge tacked on.

Traynor stepped forward. "You planning to arrest Dr. Pierce?"

Corwin glared at the man a moment. "Nah. Not yet."

"You want to take him downtown for further questioning?"

Corwin shook his head. "Maybe later."

Traynor leaned forward, putting his face close to the other man's. "Then step aside. The doctor told you he had things to do."

The two cops backed up a couple of steps and Devon strode toward the entrance.

"I'm sure we'll have more questions for you soon, Doc," Corwin called after him.

"They're just trying to get under your skin," Traynor said, keeping stride with him. "That's how they get their kicks."

Devon gave the other man a tight nod. His frustration level was out of control at the moment. He didn't trust himself to speak.

"Dr. Pierce!" Nurse Eva Bowman rushed to meet Devon in the lobby. "You're needed in the OR now. We have a gunshot victim."

Would he never get to his office? He hoped Unger didn't tire of waiting for him and walk out.

"I'll go there now," he assured Eva. "Please tell Patricia to let the man waiting to see me know that I'll only be a few minutes more."

"The man who was in your office is in OR 2," Eva explained. "He needs immediate surgery but he refuses to be put under until he speaks to you."

Devon started striding quickly toward the surgery suite before she finished speaking. "Bring me up to speed on his condition."

"When he came into your office, Ms. Ezell wasn't aware he was injured. After he'd been waiting for a bit, she went to tell him you were en route and she spotted the blood on his shirt. He was hemodynamically stable, so we imaged him. The bullet appears to have gone right through him. The bleeding is minimal, blood pressure and respiration are reasonably stable, but Dr. Frasier wants to get in there and make sure there's no damage we're not seeing."

"Let him know I'm coming and I'll scrub in."

Eva hurried into the OR while Devon made quick work of scrubbing and donning a sterile gown and gloves. He pushed his way through the door and moved toward the team surrounding the patient.

"His vitals are still stable, Dr. Pierce," Marissa Frasier said, "but we're wasting valuable time."

Unger tried to lift his head. A nurse rested her hand on his shoulder and he relaxed.

"Dr. Pierce," Unger said, his voice unsteady with pain. "I got into a little trouble before I could get to you." He stared up at the bright surgical lights, blinked rapidly and swallowed, the effort visible along the column of his throat. "I don't know what happened to my phone."

"Who did this?" Devon asked.

Unger swallowed again, then licked his lips. "I don't know for sure. What I do know for certain is that Richard learned the truth. He was trying to stop..." He coughed. "I think he was too late."

"Pressure is dropping," said Dr. Raiford, the anesthesiologist.

"I need to do this." Frasier looked to Devon. He nodded. To Unger, he said, "We'll talk again when you're well."

Devon stepped out of the OR, peeled off his gloves and gown and then entered the observation area. He lowered the privacy shield and watched for a few minutes as Frasier began the exploratory. Unger was certain Richard was innocent in this despicable mess. Perhaps Bella's assessment that Mariah was the one behind all of it was on target.

He should call Bella and tell her what Unger had said. He walked out of the observation area. No. What he should do is go back to Clark Street and demand that Mariah tell him the truth.

If the woman he had known for nearly two decades was that dangerous, Bella needed backup. He should be there with Bella.

Traynor caught up with him in the corridor. "What now, Doc?"

"Take me back to join Ms. Lytle. I believe her conclusions about Mariah Sutter are far closer to the truth than we realized."

Devon hurried to his office to advise Patricia that he would be out the remainder of the day only to find Corwin and Hodge waiting for him.

"I thought of some more of those questions

I needed to ask you," Corwin said. He jerked his head toward Devon's office. "Maybe we should talk in private, seeing that these things shouldn't be discussed in front of a lady."

Frustration hammering at him now, Devon gestured to his office. "Make yourselves comfortable. I'll be right there."

When the two detectives had done as he asked, he turned to Traynor. "You should go back to the stakeout with Bel—Ms. Lytle. I'll be fine here."

Traynor shook his head. "I'm afraid that's not the way it works, Doc. You're the client who needs protection. Trust me, Lytle can take care of herself."

Devon stepped in toe to toe with him. "You look like a tough guy to me, Mr. Traynor."

He shrugged without backing away a centimeter. "I've been called worse."

"Unless you leave this facility right now and provide whatever backup Ms. Lytle needs, I will have security take you there, leaving me as well as this facility unsecured."

Traynor backed off, held up his hands. "No need to get riled up, Doc. I got the message."

"Then go."

Devon turned his back on the man and walked into his office—his retreat—that felt more like a lion's den at the moment.

Chapter Thirteen

Clark Street, 2:30 p.m.

Bella closed the journal.

She'd reread all the entries related to Cara's lover. She was even more certain now that the unnamed lover was Mariah Sutter—not her husband, Richard. According to Unger, Richard was attempting to sort things out, which likely meant he suspected his wife as well.

Traynor had called and explained what happened with Unger. He'd warned Devon again that Richard had discovered the truth but that it was too late. Bella wasn't sure what that part meant. Had some aspect of Mariah's plan already been set in motion? Bella's first thought was an attack on the Edge facility. For that reason, Bella had insisted that Traynor stay right where he was and start a quiet search of the facility. Since Devon was tied up in his office with the detectives, Traynor did as she asked.

Bella couldn't see the point in Mariah going after Devon's home. He was rarely there and it meant little to him compared to his commitment to the Edge. The Edge was his baby—his entire focus. If Mariah Sutter really wanted to hurt him, she would hit him there. Traynor was calling in another Colby investigator who specialized in explosives. He would coordinate with Chicago PD's bomb squad if he found anything suspicious or if any threats were received.

Movement in the driveway of the Sutter home drew Bella's full attention. She watched as Mariah hurried to her Lexus and climbed behind the wheel. Bella eased down in her seat as the sedan rolled out of the drive and onto the street with hardly a pause to check for traffic.

Bella gave her a moment and then eased from between the two parallel-parked cars and merged into traffic. She kept an eye on the back of Mariah's car. Bella made the same turn onto 144th Street, followed by another turn onto Halsted and then 147th.

"Where are you going, Mariah?" Bella braked and accelerated to stay with the flow of traffic while simultaneously avoiding getting any closer to the Lexus.

They moved onto the interstate ramp and Bella leaned forward as she matched her speed to the other vehicle. For the next few miles, she tried to relax. Loosened her fingers on the wheel and considered the possibilities. Maybe she was going to meet Richard. If Unger could be believed, Richard had discovered the truth, which could very well mean there was about to be a showdown between husband and wife.

Bella hoped they were on the verge of finding an ending for Devon. He deserved to be able to go on with his life. His existence since his wife's death could hardly be called living. What Bella had felt with him last night had been real. Last night had been about pleasure and need, not about pain and punishment.

The idea that they would both likely be moving on when this was over saddened her. She knew better than to get emotionally involved with a client and yet here she was, completely wrapped up in him.

Mariah merged toward I-80 West and Bella knew exactly where she was going.

The cottage.

The drive to the cottage in Ottawa was a long one. Bella had time to allow this to play out a bit before she jumped to conclusions and alerted Devon and Traynor.

Mariah's sedan settled into a lane and stayed put. Bella did the same a few cars back. Had Richard found out about the cottage as well and demanded that she meet him there? He definitely wasn't out of the country. Maybe he'd given his wife that story so he could sit back and watch what she would do with him gone. He may have had Unger following her movements.

Still, if Mariah was the one, what had made her decide to stir this pot after all these years? Her husband was the one who'd suffered through a life-threatening disease. Even that had been some time ago, nearly three years. What had occurred to tear open the old wounds and prompt her to seek revenge or whatever it was she wanted from Devon?

The Sutters certainly weren't in any financial trouble. The motive remained a mystery. And there was always a motive.

Forty minutes later, there was no longer a question about where Mariah was headed. She took the exit into Ottawa. Bella made the call. First, she tried Devon's number, but there was no answer. Then she called Traynor.

"Hey, what's going on? I couldn't reach Dr. Pierce."

"The two detectives from the PD have had him in his office for better than an hour."

A frown furrowed its way across her brow. She moved into the right lane. "Has something new happened?"

"They found a copy of his late wife's diary at the scene where the house manager was murdered."

"Damn." The journal had nothing to do with what was happening, but it cast doubt on Devon's relationship with his wife. "They're trying to rattle him in hopes of learning something they don't know."

Sometimes when the police had nowhere to go on a case, they circled around until something or someone broke. Bella doubted very seriously that Devon Pierce would be the someone who would break for them. They were wasting their time and his.

"The facility is clear so far. McAllister brought his dog. If there's anything here, we'll find it."

"Tell McAllister I owe him one." Bella was immensely grateful the Colby Agency had Ted McAllister on their team. Ted had spent years serving in the military, most of that time as an explosives expert. Both he and the dog in his unit had lost a leg and were forced to retire. The paperwork had been endless and the frustration monumental, but McAllister had managed to get permission to take the dog home with him. Polly, a German shepherd, was loved by everyone at the agency.

"I'll give Pierce's secretary a heads-up and then I'll be right behind you."

Bella caught herself when she would have urged him to stay with Devon. She was no fool. Following a suspect into a trap was always a possibility. As badly as she wanted to simultaneously prove Mariah was behind all this and to keep Devon safe, she wanted to stay alive.

"Make sure McAllister stays close."

"You got it. Be careful, Lytle. This woman, Mariah, sounds like one twisted lady."

"Will do."

Traynor was more right than he knew. If Bella had Mariah pegged accurately, she had murdered at least two people—possibly three if that driver's body showed up—and injured two others.

Mariah and Cara had been madly in love. Bella was certain of it. The two had made major plans about the future—a home, a child. They wanted it all. Cara's death had stolen that future from Mariah. But why wait nearly seven years to seek revenge against the person she blamed for stealing that future? And why not just kill Devon? Why all the games?

Bella was missing something here.

Mariah pulled into the small drive next to the cottage and emerged from her luxury car. Bella crept along hoping Mariah wouldn't look back. Bella finally drew a deep breath when the woman hurried into the house.

The vacant house for sale across the street looked like as good a place as any to hide her car. Bella pulled into the drive and eased into the carport at the rear of the small property. Once her car was out of sight, she silenced her cell, tucked it into her pocket and headed up the street.

She strolled to the third house opposite the cottage and crossed the street at the small intersection. Recalling the layout of the cottage, she decided an approach from the rear would prove the most advantageous. She darted into a backyard two houses away. The house was quiet, so hopefully no one was home.

She moved across the yard, hopped over the small white fence all the houses on this side appeared to prefer and crossed the next yard. As she reached the rickety picket fence that separated this yard from the one that was her destination, she took stock of the situation.

No voices reverberating from inside. No one passed in front of the windows.

Bella stepped over the fence and cautiously approached the rear patio. She reached the window right of the French doors first. Peeking inside, she spotted an empty kitchen. She itched to go inside but she couldn't take that risk just yet.

A door slammed loudly. Bella jumped. Had someone gone out the front door?

Glass or something on that order shattered inside. Bella held her breath and had a look through the window again.

The front door stood open. A man lay facedown in the cased opening between the kitchen and the living room. She reached for the weapon tucked at the small of her back. The man's hair was dark, peppered with gray. Could be Richard Sutter. She couldn't see his face.

A narrow river of crimson seeped from beneath him.

She had to go in.

Holding her weapon at the ready, she went to the French doors and reached for the knob. Unlocked. She eased the door open and listened.

Silence.

Slowly, she stepped into the kitchen and scanned the room.

Clear.

She moved quickly to the man on the floor. She crouched beside him, scanning the living room as she did so.

Clear.

Bella checked his carotid artery. Still alive. She tucked her weapon into her waistband and rolled him onto his back. The knife that had entered his chest was gouged deep at an odd angle where he'd fallen against it.

Not good.

His eyes were open and his mouth worked as if he were trying to tell her something.

She reached for her cell to call for help.

Pain exploded in the back of her skull.

The agony was followed by an odd silence. The man on the floor stared up at her in defeat. Pinpricks of light sparked in front of her eyes.

And then the world went dark.

Chicago Police Department, 5:10 p.m.

DEVON PACED THE interview room. Detectives Corwin and Hodge had rushed out half an hour ago and still hadn't returned.

An hour into their questioning, the two had decided it would be best if Devon accompanied them here. At first, he'd been prepared to have them escorted out of the Edge, but then they'd told him about Maynard's revised statement.

Still, he refused to ride in the back seat of their car as if he were under arrest. Since he had ridden in this morning with Bella, he'd had to borrow his colleague Dr. Frasier's car.

He stared at his cell, willed it to ring. Why the hell hadn't he heard from Bella or from Traynor?

Something was wrong.

The door opened and the two detectives waltzed in. "Sorry for the delay," Corwin said. "We were waiting for confirmation on a couple of things."

Devon stopped his pacing and stared at the two. "Say whatever you have to say. Ask whatever you intend to ask, before I lose my patience."

In truth, he already had. He'd had to fight the urge to call his attorney. If he remained cooperative, perhaps this would be over more quickly.

Not that his cooperation had helped so far.

"Sit." Corwin gestured to a chair on Devon's side of the table as he and Hodge collapsed into the ones on their side.

Hodge shuffled through a stack of pages and handed several to his partner, keeping a few for himself.

"Ms. Maynard recanted her earlier statement and provided a new one."

Devon felt the final remnants of his patience slipping from his grasp. "You mentioned this more than an hour ago and I still have no idea how this revised statement impacts me. Why am I here?"

Corwin placed a photo on the table in front of Devon. "Do you know this man?"

Devon studied the image, then shook his head. "I don't, no. Who is he?"

"This is the missing driver," Corwin explained. "The one who picked Maynard up from her street corner and drove her to meet the person who paid her to pretend to be your wife."

Devon nodded. "I see. Did you find him?"

Hodge laughed. "Oh, we found him all right. He took a bullet right through the eye." He tapped his left eye. "It was a .32. Just like the one that killed the mechanic found in the trunk of the Lexus Maynard was driving."

Another murder. Devon's chest felt tight with the weight of yet another death. "Do you know if it was the same weapon?"

"We're checking that now," Hodge explained. "We might not know until tomorrow, but we believe that will be the case."

Richard Sutter had a couple of weapons but Devon had no idea the caliber. It wasn't something they ever really discussed, but at some point during all the years they had known each other, the subject of weapons had come up. Richard had mentioned having one in his nightstand. He also remembered Richard mentioning that Mariah and some of her friends were taking a weapons training class. Mariah had wanted Cara to attend as well.

The urge to call Bella with this news was nearly overwhelming. She should know about this. She was watching Mariah.

He checked the time again. Something was wrong. He should have heard from her by now.

"Maynard says the driver was her boyfriend. He was the one who made the deal with the person who set all this in motion," Corwin explained. "She said that she made up the other statement because she was trying to protect her boyfriend. But now that he's dead, she spilled her guts."

"You found him first and used that to get her to talk," Devon suggested. How long had these two known about the dead driver? Or Maynard's new statement? Long enough to be running ballistics on the bullet that killed the man. Fury tightened in Devon's gut.

"Does Maynard know the person who hired her?"

Corwin shook his head. "She doesn't but she does know it was a woman."

That bad feeling he'd been ignoring swelled inside him. "This person—this woman— hasn't left any evidence? A fingerprint? A hair? Anything?"

"Not that we've found so far," Hodge said, scanning another report.

"Is there a woman in your history," Corwin asked, "who might want revenge for some reason?"

The name burgeoned in his throat. He opened his mouth, ready to tell them all that he suspected regarding Mariah Sutter, but his cell vibrated.

He snatched it from his pocket and took the call without checking the screen. "Yes."

"This is Traynor."

Devon kept his attention on the two detectives. "I'm glad you called. Is everything in order?"

"Your ex-partner Richard Sutter is dead."

Devon stood, uncertainty raging through him. "What about Bella?"

"Her car is here at the cottage in Ottawa." Traynor hesitated a moment. "Her weapon is here, but she isn't."

"Thank you." Devon struggled to keep the fury and the fear twisting inside him from making an appearance. "I'll be there as soon as I can."

Devon ended the call and slid the phone back into his pocket, his movements as calm and relaxed as he could manage. "I have an emergency, gentlemen. I hope you'll keep me updated on your progress."

"Count on it." Corwin stood. "I kind of miss your lady friend. Where'd you say she was off to?"

"She's following up on an old friend of my late wife's."

Devon moved toward the door, the blood pounding in his ears.

"Be careful the secrets you keep, Dr. Pierce," Corwin called after him. "They can get people killed."

Chapter Fourteen

Devon made it outside without breaking into a run. He found Frasier's car and dropped behind the steering wheel. He dug for his cell, selected the contact for Mariah and then started the car.

He had merged into traffic by the time she answered. That she answered at all startled him.

"I wondered how long it would take you to call, Devon."

A searing anger blazed through him, banishing the shock. He fought hard to muster a reasonably calm voice. "What the hell are you doing, Mariah? Richard is dead. Where are you?"

Deep breath. Don't let her hear your fear.

"What? You're not even going to ask about your new friend? I saw the way you looked at her when the two of you visited my home that first time. I knew then that she was part of this, too."

A thread of sheer panic rushed through his veins. He had no idea where to go. Traynor was at the cottage. Bella wasn't there. Where would Mariah take her?

"Let's talk about this, Mariah. Tell me where to meet you. We'll work out whatever the problem is together. I'm prepared to do whatever you say."

His tone sounded reasonable, calm, though every muscle and nerve in his body strummed with bone-shattering tension.

"We're waiting for you at your home, Devon. Now, be very smart, old friend. Come alone. No police. We can settle this among ourselves, I believe. But if you force my hand, your sweet little friend will have to join Richard in hell. We both know you don't want that."

The call ended.

Devon took a breath and drove to a less busy area of the city to determine if the police were following him. He had a feeling that was the reason for the visit to the station. Otherwise the detectives could certainly have continued to interrogate him at his office. Obviously they had wanted to set up a situation and then watch his reaction. Then all they had to do was follow close behind him.

He executed a couple of turns to take him into a less traffic-heavy area. After a couple more turns, he spotted the dark sedan making all the same maneuvers. This was one time he would have preferred to be wrong.

Devon couldn't remember the last time he'd attempted to outmaneuver or outrun another vehicle. Perhaps when he was a teenager. He supposed it was never too late to determine if he possessed the necessary skills. One rapid-fire turn after the other, first right, then left, then right again, and he accelerated past a garbage truck and then veered down an alley on the left.

From there, he retraced his route via a couple of different streets and headed for the one that would take him to I-90. If he pushed the speed limit as far as he dared and still avoided being pulled over, he could make it to his house in fifty minutes.

At the next required stop, he sought and found the number for the Colby Agency. When the receptionist had transferred his call to Victoria, he explained the situation. The step was the only one he felt fully confident in taking.

"First," Victoria said, "slow down. I don't want you arriving at your home until I have people on-site."

"She warned me to come alone," he reminded his old friend. "I will not risk Bella's life by going against Mariah's demands."

"Traynor and McAllister know what they're doing, Devon," Victoria reminded him. "Sutter will not be aware they are there until they're ready for her to know."

Devon ordered his heart rate to slow. He drew in a slow, deep breath. "All right. Tell me what to do."

"I'll give you the heads-up when Traynor and McAllister are in place. Then you'll go to the house exactly as Sutter requested. Try to engage her with dialogue. People who do this have something to say. Listen. Be sympathetic. But be careful not to sound patronizing. She needs to see and feel your fear. This is real, and if she suspects that you're not worried or afraid, she'll know she's been set up."

"Very well. I'll drive the speed limit and wait for your call."

"We've got this, Devon. Keep in mind that Bella is a highly trained former detective. She knows how to take care of herself."

Devon thanked Victoria and focused on driving.

Victoria was right. Bella was more than capable. But that didn't make him feel any better about the situation. There were so many things he wanted to learn about her. For the first time in years, he wanted to feel something more than mere respect and compassion for another human being. He wanted a relationship with Bella.

He wanted to share a life with her for however long she would have him. He wanted to make her his.

Devon laughed out loud at the preposterous thought. Bella would be the first to tell him that she belonged to no one but herself. Whatever relationship they were able to build together, it would be one of mutual respect and admiration. Perhaps not completely. He wasn't sure she could ever feel the same fierce need for him that he felt for her. It was too early to label his feelings precisely, but they were strong.

For now, he wanted the opportunity to explore those feelings and every part of this fascinating woman.

If she was willing.

He refused to consider that one or both of them might die today.

Arbor Drive, Lake Bluff, 5:30 p.m.

BELLA'S EYES FLUTTERED OPEN. A distant ache throbbed in the back of her head. There was something she needed to remember.

Something she needed to do...

Mariah. Mariah Sutter.

Bella willed her body to sit up. The room

spun and her stomach churned as if she might vomit. She scrubbed her hand across her face. Her body felt as if it belonged to someone else. What the hell was wrong with her?

She tried to clear her throat...tried to swallow. Her mouth felt dry.

Where was she? She looked around. Not the cottage. She blinked until her eyes focused on the fireplace across the room.

Devon's house.

"You're awake. Good."

Bella jerked at the sound of Mariah's voice. The throb in her head deepened and she felt ready to pass out again. As if she were watching for someone, Mariah stood by the window at the end of the room that faced the front of the property.

I need the new security code.

Bella vaguely remembered hearing the question over and over. Had she given Mariah the code? She must have. Devon had changed it after his house manager's murder. Mariah couldn't have known it otherwise. Now she remembered. The blow to her head had rattled her. She probably had a concussion considering she'd been unconscious for a bit. Mariah had disarmed her, roused her and forced her into the car she'd been driving.

Richard was dead.

Mariah had killed him.

The bitter taste in Bella's mouth made her want to gag. She suppressed the reflex. Mariah had given her something. A drug.

She squeezed her eyes shut and shook her head. The pain in her skull throbbed.

"Don't worry. I didn't give you very much. It should be almost worn off by now." Mariah strolled toward the sofa Bella had been lying on. "Liquid morphine. The pills weren't really working for me. The doctors want me to be comfortable at this stage. The past couple of days have been hell. I didn't expect the pain to become so bad so quickly."

Bella licked her lips. "You're dying," she guessed.

A weary sigh echoed from the other woman. "That's what they tell me. Frankly, until a couple of days ago, I secretly hoped they'd made a mistake. The pain is no fun, but the disease hasn't really slowed me down until lately. I swear to God, when that fool Harper tried to kill me with her damned butcher knife, I thought she might succeed. All I needed was the key and the security code to the house. Who knew she would go shopping without her list and have to come back for it. I didn't want to kill her but she left me no choice."

"Why did you do any of this?" Bella asked.

The longer she could keep the woman talking and distracted, the more time she would have for shaking the effects of the drug.

"They stole everything from me," she said without hesitation. "Richard took my youth. Refused to have children. And then he had the audacity to try to seduce Cara. She came to me and cried. She was so certain it was her fault. We ended up crying together. One thing turned into another, and the next thing we knew, we were making love." She walked back to the window and stared out. "I have never loved anyone the way I loved Cara. We had everything planned. Then Richard got sick and we agreed that I should see him through that hard time." She shook her head. "That was our mistake. If we'd walked out as planned, we would have had all this time together."

Bella used the arm of the sofa and pulled to her feet. She swayed.

"When he was finally back on his feet again, Cara and I resumed our plans. Everything was arranged. She wanted to get away from Chicago for a week or so after breaking the news to Devon. I was to join her in New York after he left. Only none of that ever happened. First, Richard found out and went ballistic. He made all sorts of threats, but we got through that one. Then there was the accident." Her voice drifted off.

"But you stayed with Richard anyway," Bella said, braced against the end of the sofa. She wasn't quite steady enough to trust herself to rush across the room and tackle the woman. Hopefully she would get there soon.

Was Mariah armed? She no doubt had Bella's weapon.

"I was too devastated to do anything else," Mariah went on, seeming to talk more to herself than to Bella. "I couldn't sleep or eat. It was as if my life had ended, too. Really, I suppose it had. The only difference was that I was still breathing. Richard and Devon started to have trouble and suddenly Richard was determined to destroy Devon's career. For a time, that was enough. Then last year, I received my own death sentence. Lung cancer. The worst kind. Something snapped inside me." She shrugged, her expression distant. "I realized that men like Richard and Devon had stolen the past as well as the future I deserved—that Cara and I deserved. And I was furious."

She stared out the window again and Bella tested her legs once more. One slow step at a time, she moved to the other sofa, just ten or so feet, but it was something. She leaned against it as she had the other sofa.

"It must have taken a great deal of planning to set up such an elaborate plan." Bella needed her talking again. "Why not just kill him? It would have been so much easier."

"Because killing him wasn't enough!" Mariah said, her voice vibrating with emotion. "You can't imagine. Within days of learning I was dying, I started to plan. Before I killed either one of them, I wanted to make Devon suffer. To question his own sanity. And if nasty rumors about him started circulating and ruined his hospital—his *baby*—even better."

"Using the Cara look-alike was ingenious," Bella offered. "But did you have to kill the driver and the mechanic?"

"Men are so stupid." Mariah reached beneath her jacket and withdrew a .32. "The mechanic tried to back out on me after I'd paid him so handsomely. The driver, as it turns out, was Maynard's pimp boyfriend and he tried to demand more money." She laughed. "Killing them was practice. I'd never murdered anyone before. I wanted to make sure I could do it. A dress rehearsal."

"I guess Unger was lucky, then, since he survived." Bella's head had stopped spinning. The pain was worse but at least she could think clearly and stand upright without swaying.

"I had every intention of killing the little bastard. I caught him in my house. He was trying to find evidence of what I was up to for Richard. Richard had his suspicions but he couldn't prove a damned thing. The only thing he could do was stay hidden so I wouldn't kill him first. Coward."

"So now you're going to kill Devon, is that it?" Bella wished for water.

Mariah cocked her head and eyed Bella. "I can't stomach the thought of him living one day more than I do. So, yes, I'm going to kill Devon. But first, I'm going to kill you. Like Harper, I really don't want to hurt you, but I have to use whatever is at my disposal to get the job done."

Bella made a face of confusion. "What did I do? I was only hired to help him figure out what was going on. I had nothing to do with taking Cara from you or the cancer eating away at your lungs."

Mariah smiled. "You were a surprise. I wasn't worried when he hired your agency. I was confident in my plan and the steps I'd taken to cover my tracks. But when I saw the two of you together that first time, I knew I'd been given the coup de grâce. He has feelings for you. Maybe not the kind of feelings I had for Cara but something. So before I kill him, I'm going to take you away from him. He deserves to know how that feels. He should be here any moment."

Bella didn't have a lot of time. Traynor would have figured out she was in trouble and be working on some kind of backup. Apparently Mariah had given Devon their location. If Devon was smart, and Bella knew he was, he would have called Traynor or Victoria.

Mariah's plan had failed already.

As true as that most likely was, Bella understood the variables in any operation's projected outcome. Something could always go wrong and someone could end up dead. She had no weapon. She'd been drugged and the effects weren't completely worn off. The odds were not stacked in her favor.

But she'd never been a quitter and she wasn't about to start now.

"See," Mariah said with a glance out the window. "I knew he'd come alone." She sent a sinister look at Bella. "He does care about you. Otherwise he would have stayed in his office and sent the police to handle the matter."

Bella braced for making some sort of move. Devon likely knew he was walking into a trap. If Mariah took some time to taunt him, it would give Bella more of a chance to make a move.

Mariah watched as Devon emerged from the car.

It was now or never.

Bella ran. She was barefoot, so she made it several yards before Mariah realized she had moved.

"Stop! Or I'll shoot!"

Bella darted through the cased opening and into the dining room. True to her word, Mariah fired off a shot.

Bella cut through the kitchen and raced into the entry hall just as Devon was opening the front door.

"Out!" she shouted. "Go back out!"

Devon dived for her.

They hit the floor.

Two shots exploded in the entry hall, echoing like thunder.

Bella's head was spinning again. The room tilted.

Another shot fired. This one shattered the glass in the door.

Devon scrambled to his feet and charged Mariah.

Bella scrambled onto all fours. She launched herself up and rushed to where Mariah and Devon struggled.

Mariah still had the weapon. Devon forced her hand and the .32 away from his head. The weapon fired.

Bella jerked at the sound as the bullet plowed into the plaster wall.

Traynor and McAllister barged into the room.

The next pull of the trigger was followed by a hollow sound. Mariah had fired her final round.

Traynor snatched the weapon from her hand and Devon got to his feet. McAllister subdued her with a pair of nylon cuffs. Despite knowing she'd lost and that her game was over, she ranted and railed about getting Devon one way or the other.

Bella leaned against the wall. She couldn't remember when she'd felt so tired.

"Are you all right?" Devon surveyed her as if terrified that she was gravely injured.

Bella managed a smile. "I'll live. She hit me in the head with something and then drugged me with morphine." She met his gaze. "She's dying. Lung cancer."

Mariah had lapsed into sobs. Sirens were blaring outside.

Devon demanded, "Let me have a look at you."

While the police came in and removed Mariah Sutter, Devon examined the back of Bella's head and checked her eyes and reflexes.

"I'm taking you to the Edge," he said when

he'd finished. "I want a full workup. A traumatic brain injury is nothing to scoff at."

"I'm fine, really," she argued. There was no need to make a fuss.

Devon disregarded everything she said. He answered a few questions for the officer as Mariah was escorted out. He promised that he and Bella would come in tomorrow and make official statements.

"Go," Traynor said when Devon looked to him. "McAllister and I will take care of things here."

"This really isn't necessary," Bella tried again.

"Listen to the doc," Traynor ordered.

McAllister folded his beefy arms over his chest. "Don't make one of us have to carry you out of here."

Bella rolled her eyes and relented. "Fine." She turned to Devon. "Let's get this over with."

The Edge, 10:00 p.m.

DR. FRASIER STUDIED the monitor. Devon stared over her shoulder.

Bella exhaled a big breath, hoping they would hear it and realize she was waiting. When they both continued to stare at the monitor and talk quietly to one another, she said, "Well?"

"The concussion is mild," Dr. Frasier said as she turned to Bella. "You'll need someone seeing after you for a few days. If you have a headache that gets worse or any weakness, numbness or—"

"I'll be taking care of her," Devon interrupted. "I know the warning signs to watch for." To Bella, he said, "It's important that you're not alone. No driving or overexertion for at least forty-eight hours."

Bella hugged her arms around herself and the unflattering hospital gown she'd had to change into for the MRI. "Yay me."

Dr. Frasier smiled warmly. "Don't worry. Most of the time, symptoms don't linger for more than a few days. I'll write your discharge order." She left the room.

"We could take a vacation."

Bella looked up at him. "A vacation?" She held her breath. Where was he going with that?

He leaned against the table next to her, tucked a wisp of hair behind her ear with one long finger. "The business part of our relationship is over now."

"I still have to do my final report," she argued.

"I'm certain Victoria would understand if your report was delayed."

Her heart wouldn't stop pounding. She needed

to think. To reason this all out. "But you have so much to do here. How can they possibly run this place without you?"

He traced the swell of her cheek. "I have complete confidence in my staff, and the truth is, I've recently realized that I need more than work."

"What is it you want to do, Dr. Pierce?"

She didn't want to read too much into this. Stressful situations—life-and-death ones in particular—often made people reach out to one another. Then, when the stressor had passed, those passions faded. She had no desire to make more of this than it was.

"I want to be with you," he said bluntly. "I want to know you—all of you. I want to begin right now. This minute."

She smiled as his lips brushed hers. "But we're in the ER."

He straightened, backed away from her. All the way to the door. He locked it.

Her heart skipped a beat. "I thought I wasn't supposed to overexert myself or something like that."

He walked the few feet back to where she sat on the exam table. Just watching him move made her pulse react. "You don't have to do anything but enjoy. Besides, I'm a doctor. I can take care of any situation that arises. Trust me."

He spread her legs and moved between them. "Aren't there rules against this behavior with a patient?" she teased.

He kissed that sensitive skin beneath her ear. "You're not *my* patient."

She shivered with the feel of his breath against the damp skin.

"I want to take you away from here." He left a kiss along her jawline between each word. "Make love to you every day and every night for as long as you're willing."

His lips brushed her collarbone and she shook with pleasure. "As soon as I'm well enough," she countered.

He drew back. Studied her flushed face. "Of course." His hand worked its way beneath her gown and up to her bare breast. He squeezed. "How are you feeling now?"

She whimpered. "Good."

He moved on to the other breast and massaged her nipple between his fingers. Pleasure shot through her.

"Good?" he asked.

"Oh yes."

His hand slid down her rib cage, fingers reaching between her thighs, finding that damp heat that yearned for his touch. He pressed his mouth to her ear and whispered all the ways he intended to make her come as his fingers worked their magic. His free arm went around her waist, held her steady as he brought her closer and closer to orgasm. Then he gripped her tight and finished sending her over the edge.

She bit her lips together to prevent crying out with the pleasure that pulsed through her. Blindly, she reached for his fly, but he gently pushed her hands away. "Later," he murmured. "This was just a taste of all the ways I'm going to make you come apart in my arms."

She grinned. "You know what they say about payback."

"I look forward to it." He reached for the bag at the end of the table. "Now let's get you dressed so I can take you out of here."

He helped her dress. They laughed when she swayed and kissed when they couldn't bear not to. It felt good. It felt right.

"I'm suddenly starving," she said as he slipped her shoes on her feet.

"I know a place not far from here that stays open until midnight. You good with Italian?"

"I love Italian."

When he held her hand as they walked out of the room, Bella's chest filled to bursting. It wasn't the let-me-help-you kind of touch. It was the I-want-to-hold-your-hand touch.

They spoke to the nurses and to Dr. Frasier

as they left. It was as if he wanted them all to see that they were together. She liked that he didn't try to hide what he was feeling.

Outside, they walked slowly in the cool night air to his car. He'd had a driver pick up the one he'd borrowed, fill the gas tank and return it to Dr. Frasier. Traynor had told her that even before he and McAllister left the Lake Bluff house someone had been there, making the needed repairs after Mariah's shooting spree.

Devon opened her door and helped her into the car. By the time she fastened her seat belt, he was sliding behind the wheel.

"Where are we going on this vacation?" she asked, though she didn't really care. She would gladly go anywhere with him.

"Where would you like to go?"

She thought about that for a moment, then turned his question on him. "Where would *you* like to go?"

He backed out of the slot and paused to look at her. "Anywhere, as long as you're there."

She laughed. "I was just thinking the same thing."

Chapter Fifteen

The Edge, Sunday, June 10, 2:00 p.m.

"You have a second-degree burn, Mr. Camp," Dr. Frasier announced.

Victoria sent Lucas a pointed look. "Told you so."

Lucas sighed, his expression downtrodden. "Yes, you did. What's the plan, Dr. Frasier?"

Dr. Frasier smiled. "It's not that bad, Mr. Camp. I'm sure you know that with a second-degree burn the damage extends a little deeper than the top layer of skin. The area is already red and sensitive but you will most likely see blistering as well. How did you say you burned yourself?"

"The barbecue grill," he confessed. "It's a biweekly ritual during the summer."

Victoria squeezed her dear husband's uninjured hand. "Only this time, someone wasn't paying attention."

As Lucas and Dr. Frasier chatted about the steps that would be taken, which weren't so bad—cleaning and applying an antibiotic and then bandaging—Victoria thought of how frightened she had been when she'd watched him reach for the veggie basket without the protection of an oven mitt. At their age, it wasn't unusual on occasion to forget where you left the keys or to forget what you walked into a room to look for, but to forget to protect your hand when you reached for a hot item and then to hang on to it until you moved it to the counter was outside the boundaries of acceptable. She would be watching her dear husband closely going forward.

Her heart ached at even the mere thought of what this could mean.

Victoria pushed away the painful idea. "I understand Devon and Bella made it safely to Saint-Tropez."

Frasier smiled. "They did."

Lucas gave her a wink. "I hear you're in charge while he's gone."

She laughed. "I am. Dr. Pierce hasn't designated a deputy administrator, so I'm it for now. Well, with Ms. Ezell's support, of course. She runs that office anyway."

Victoria knew well that there was nothing

more valuable than a top-notch secretary or personal assistant. "I'm certain you'll do fine."

"Thank you." The doctor gave Lucas a pat on the shoulder. "Mr. Camp, I'll have Nurse Bowman come in and take care of you. Just keep the injured area clean. Apply an antibiotic cream once a day and keep it bandaged for a few days and you'll be as good as new before you know it."

"Thanks, Dr. Frasier."

Forty-five minutes later, they were headed home. The white bandage was stark against her husband's tanned hand.

"Lucas, I'm worried about you."

He turned to her, watched her for a while. Victoria kept her gaze on the street and traffic.

"In what way, my dear? The burn isn't so bad."

He wasn't going to like this very much. "You picked up the pan without an oven mitt and you held it for several seconds—long enough to move it—before you let go."

"Not such a smart move," he agreed. "I wasn't thinking." He reached over and patted her hand with his good one. "I assure you it was nothing more. Just an absentminded moment that I will regret for at least a week or so."

She hoped that was the case. "You haven't

had any other similar moments that you haven't told me about, have you?"

"I certainly have not."

Victoria felt some amount of relief at hearing him say so. Still, her heart ached with worry.

"Do you want the truth?" he asked.

She glanced at her husband. "I not only want it, I expect it!" What sort of question was that?

"We have a rather important anniversary coming up."

Twenty years. Victoria's smile was automatic. She and Lucas had been married for almost twenty years.

"I've been planning this very special getaway. I was actually considering Saint-Tropez. I thought I would ask Bella when she returns if it was as wonderful as the rumors suggest. At any rate, I'm found out now."

"Lucas, that sounds lovely." She reached over and placed a hand on his leg. "I'd love to go to Saint-Tropez."

"You're always arranging things for others, Victoria," he said. "I wanted to do this for you—for us. I wanted it to be a surprise."

She reached for his hand and entwined her fingers with his. "It's a lovely surprise. I'm so pleased."

"I was only distracted and not paying attention." He squeezed her fingers. "I will tell you if I ever feel there's something not quite right about any part of me."

"Is that a promise?"

"It is."

"Good." She exhaled a big breath. "I won't worry anymore, then."

This was, of course, not entirely true, but she would try.

"While you were taking care of the paperwork, Eva Bowman told me a troubling story about Dr. Frasier."

Victoria took the next turn. "So you were gossiping with your nurse," she teased.

"I certainly was. Eva is worried about Dr. Frasier. Apparently her former husband has given her trouble from time to time. He's just out of prison after a one-year stretch for felony domestic violence."

"Was Dr. Frasier the victim?"

"Unfortunately."

"Has she seen someone about a restraining order?" Not that a mere restraining order would stop the determined. But it made things simpler when the police were called.

"She has not. Eva said she'd already urged Dr. Frasier to take that step. She also gave her our number and suggested she consider calling us."

"I hope she will."

"I think I'll have Jamie do some research," Lucas said. "Find out who this guy is and where he is."

"Excellent idea. If Dr. Frasier needs us, we'll be prepared."

"Speaking of Jamie," Lucas said, "did you know she has a new boyfriend?"

"Did she tell you this?" Victoria sent him a sideways glance. She was utterly envious that he'd heard this news before she had.

"I saw it on one of her social-media pages."

Victoria frowned. "Are you monitoring our granddaughter's accounts again?"

"I'm one of her newest friends, Lucky Luke."

Victoria laughed. "Lucky Luke?"

"Why not? I'm the luckiest man alive because you're my wife."

Victoria braked for a light and turned to him. "You are so charming, Lucas. We're both very lucky." She grinned. "What does this young man look like?"

The light changed and she rolled forward with the flow of traffic.

"Tall and handsome, of course. He's a senior at the University of Chicago."

"Have you looked into him and his family?"

"The boy's pedigree is noteworthy. I'm sure you will approve."

Victoria sighed. "Time is traveling far too fast, Lucas."

"It is." He squeezed her hand once more. "We've seen and done so much, been through so much. But, good God, what a ride."

This was true. Victoria smiled. So very true.

* * * * *

Don't miss the next installment of the
COLBY AGENCY: SEXI-ER
coming next month!
Look for BODY OF EVIDENCE
from Debra Webb and Harlequin Intrigue.

Get 4 FREE REWARDS!

We'll send you 2 FREE Books plus 2 FREE Mystery Gifts.

Harlequin Presents® books feature a sensational and sophisticated world of international romance where sinfully tempting heroes ignite passion.

FREE
Value Over
$20